THE ONLY ONE

A ROMANCE

SOMI EKHASOMHI

SWEET ACACIA PRESS

This is a work of fiction. Names, characters, businesses, places, events and incidents are the products of the author's imagination or used in a fictitious manner. Any resemblance to actual persons, living or dead, or actual events is purely coincidental.

To M and J...
My world...
Every day by day.

CHAPTER ONE

THERE WAS ALMOST no part of Victoria Island where parking wasn't a problem. Hope Alade's office was no exception. Fifteen floors of offices and yet, only the ground floor for parking. After securing a spot in the morning, it was the most reckless thing to risk it by driving out to lunch. Which was what Hope had done.

The uniformed security man shook his head again, squinting as the hot sun reflected off his shiny forehead. "Parking don full," he said, his voice heavy with sober finality, which would have been amusing, except Hope wasn't in the mood to laugh. "Aunty Hope, you go park for street."

"Ohhhhh!" Hope dragged out a long groan before backing away from the gate and finding a space on the street in front of the building. She disliked parking on the street. It never felt safe. There was always the risk of reckless drivers scratching her car, or worse, the people from the traffic agency appearing out of nowhere to seize and tow cars.

Hope's colleague, Agnes Disu, lay reclining on the passenger seat, her eyes heavy. "Give him your keys so as soon as someone leaves, he'll move the car inside," she murmured, still drowsy from loading up on pounded yam and Port-Harcourt native soup.

"It's not like I have a choice," Hope said, abandoning her contemplation of Agnes to glance up and down the street. There were other cars parked along the curb, but that didn't make her feel better. "I hate leaving my car on the street," she muttered. "We should have walked."

Agnes rolled her eyes. "Walk ke! So we'll arrive at a restaurant full of big boys with my skin sweaty and makeup running down my face." Her lips pursed. "Thank you very much, but no thank you."

Hope chuckled. Agnes was obsessed with big boys, fine boys, hot boys, or just boys. In the two years they had worked together at Madueke and Makinde Engineering, she had come to realise that while Agnes was sharp as a new needle at things like circuit diagrams and specifications for electrical fittings, with men, especially cute ones, she was as hopeless as a teenager in the throes of her first crush.

"How many big boys did you catch while you were loading pounded yam?" Hope laughed, shaking her head. She turned off the engine and stepped out of the car and into the unforgiving Lagos sun. The heat enveloped her like a malicious evil spirit, and she grimaced, thinking how the interior of her car would be as hot as an oven in a matter of minutes.

"I didn't catch any because I couldn't concentrate," Agnes said, after pulling herself out of the passenger seat. She patted her stomach and sighed. She had an undeniably sensual kind of beauty, large eyes, full lips, and a smooth creamy complexion that gleamed in the sun.

She grinned at Hope. "...And, I couldn't concentrate because I was still thinking of the one I saw in our office right before we left for lunch."

Which one was that? Hope searched her memory. She wasn't as giddy as Agnes when it came to men, but she wasn't averse to enjoying the sight of a good-looking one either. She couldn't remember seeing any extraordinarily handsome guys in the office before they'd left for lunch.

Walking ahead of Agnes, she strode inside the compound and gave her car keys to the security man, giving him instructions to move the car inside as there was space.

"I don't know how you could have missed him," Agnes said breathlessly, when she caught up with Hope. "He came in right before we went out for lunch, tall, handsome, smooth... with lips like sugar."

"Lips like sugar?" Hope burst out laughing. "I give up on you, Agnes. You're just man crazy."

"Which one is man crazy again?" Agnes rolled her eyes. Even in her four-inch heels she was still at least half a foot closer to the ground than Hope, curvy, with a full head of curly hair extensions. In contrast, Hope was slender and tall, with a weakness for long, wavy hair extensions that blended perfectly with her relaxed hair. She was good looking, with a clear bronze complexion and dark expressive eyes.

Beyond the impressive revolving doors, the lobby of the Matador house was an air-conditioned cave of marble floors and walls, with busy-looking professionals heading to and from their offices.

"This Lagos sun is enough to kill somebody sha," Agnes said. "Just from the street to the lobby and I'm already sweating." She glanced at Hope. "And just so you know. It is perfectly normal for a girl my age to be man-crazy. If I weren't, even my parents would be worried."

"Now, I'm sure they're worried that you've taken it a little too far," Hope replied with a snort.

Agnes laughed. "Free me, abeg."

The engineering services firm where they worked was on one of the upper floors. They headed toward the lifts, and Hope slowed her stride so Agnes could keep up. There was no rush, for Hope at least. She was far ahead of all her deadlines. She enjoyed her work, and while the endless diagrams and schematic drawing of the intestines of buildings were boring to some people, they weren't to her.

"You should have seen him," Agnes declared, returning to the subject of the mysterious hot guy, "He came just before lunch for a meeting with one of the managing partners. He was hot. Tall, team light-skinned with dimples," she winked at Hope. "and have I mentioned the lips?"

Hope sighed. "Yeah," she said tiredly. "Lips like sugar."

"Exactly!" Agnes sighed dramatically.

The description nagged at Hope's mind, like a feather tickling at a memory. She knew one person who looked like that, or at least as close to Agnes's exaggerated descriptions as she could imagine. And he was the last person she expected or desired to see in her office.

Luckily, there were probably thousands of guys who looked like that in Victoria Island.

A lift descended, and the doors slid open. They stepped inside, and Agnes continued her monologue, her eyes shining as she described the perfection of the mysterious guy. Hope listened, her feelings vacillating between amusement and boredom.

The lift had barely moved when it came to a stop on the second floor. Agnes continued her chattering until the doors opened and Daniel Amadi walked in.

That shut her up.

That would have shut anybody up. Nobody would dream of chattering brainlessly when a man like Daniel Amadi was in the same room.

Every single person in the building knew who he was...the genius software engineer who built his business from scratch, and whose offices occupied the top three floors of the building.

There was something about the way he strode into the lift in his impeccable dark suit and crisp white shirt. There was something about the set of his jaw, the understated glint of his silver cufflinks, the subtle hint of his cologne... It was as if, just with the way he carried himself, he was proclaiming that he owned the place.

He acknowledged them with a small nod. He never gave anybody more than that. He probably believed he didn't need to give any additional acknowledgement to two random engineers from the small firm a few floors below him, Hope thought unimpressed.

As the doors closed, he turned his back to them and faced the panel. At first, Hope watched his long fingers moving over the buttons, but then Agnes caught her attention, rolling her eyes upwards and fanning her chest in a mimicry of swooning. Hope stuck out her tongue and stifled a giggle.

Daniel turned back towards them, missing the moment of hilarity. He wasn't smiling. In fact, Hope doubted that she had ever seen him smile. She had never really understood why all the girls in the office thought he walked on water. He was always serious, and he always looked busy. Sure, he was handsome, in that tall, dark and intense way that would have looked good in a model, but what was the use of all the good looks if he never cracked a smile?

The lift was moving. Hope glanced at Agnes, who was staring at the side of Daniel Amadi's face like a child discovering a glowing, colourful screen for the first time. She stifled another giggle.

The silence was getting uncomfortable, and now Hope could feel him looking at her. Why was the lift so sluggish? It felt as if his eyes were burning through her skin.

She looked up at him and caught him mid-stare. If he was fazed at getting caught, he didn't show it. Dark eyes, ringed with thick black lashes, lingered on her face for a moment, and then flickered away.

Hope remembered to breathe. In that one moment, she'd felt almost...lost in the force of his gaze. Flashes of warmth touched the surface of her skin. "...seven, eight, nine..." She counted the numbers under her breath as they appeared on the indicator. For some reason she couldn't articulate, she could hardly wait to put some distance... and breathing space... between herself and Daniel Amadi.

She heard a clatter and almost jumped out of her skin. The sound was from her small purse, which had slipped from her fingers and fallen on the floor.

In the few moments it took for her to make that realisation, Daniel Amadi had dropped gracefully to his haunches and retrieved the tiny pink purse. Hope stood frozen as he rose to his feet and handed it to her.

"Here," he said quietly. There was nothing personal or friendly about his deep voice. She could have been any clumsy old lady, judging from his expressionless face.

"Thank you," Hope whispered, reaching out with wooden fingers to take the purse. Thankfully, she grasped it without immediately dropping it again.

"You're welcome, Hope." He smiled but didn't let go of the purse.

Hope forgot that they were both holding her purse, that there was something wrong with that, that it looked awkward. She forgot all that because...What a smile! The curve of his lips, the stark whiteness of his teeth, the amused gleam in his eyes...it was almost...mesmerising.

And how come he knew her name? Hope stared at him in surprise as the doors slowly slid open.

One eyebrow went up on his face, and his eyes, still slightly amused, remained on hers, like he knew what she was thinking.

Hope stared, forgetting where she was supposed to be going. When he released her purse, she stared at him for a few more moments, slightly disoriented. She caught herself and walked out of the lift, her legs unsteady as she wondered what had just happened.

CHAPTER TWO

IT WAS STILL lunchtime when Hope and Agnes walked through a set of glass doors with the words Madueke and Makinde Engineering etched in thick white letters.

At the front desk, one of the receptionists, Joy, was flipping disinterestedly through a travel magazine. The other receptionist, Ladi, who usually pulled her status as a senior employee, and older, married woman, had gone to lunch first. She'd no doubt arrive close to the end of the lunch break, leaving Joy only a few minutes to rush through her own lunch.

Agnes hurried past Hope on her high heels, to the marble and glass reception desk.

"Aw, sweetie, you've still not gone to lunch." She took the magazine from Joy. "What is this one you're reading sef?" Not waiting for an answer, she tossed the magazine aside. "If only you had come out with us, then I won't have been the only witness to Hope and Daniel Amadi flirting in the lift."

"Flir...what!" Joy's face lost the boredom in an instant. She looked at Hope with a gleam in her eyes that could either have been respect or envy. "Serious?!"

Hope chuckled. "Don't mind Agnes. He only said *hello*."

"He said hello to you?" Apparently, that was as much of a big deal as the flirting that hadn't happened. "But he doesn't say hello to *anybody*!"

Come to think of it, had he even said hello? Seeing the expression on Joy's face, Hope felt a morbid fear of seeing her picture in some gossip blog or the other. BREAKING! Rich and Eligible Lagos bachelor Daniel Amadi says hello to boring engineer.

"It wasn't like that...we were in the lift together." Hope looked at Agnes for help. "He didn't even say hello, he just...acknowledged us a little."

"Us?" Agnes pursed her lips. "Don't mind Hope o! I was there, her purse fell, and he picked it up for her."

Joy's eyes widened to almost twice their regular size, but Agnes had not finished. "Then they started looking deep into each other's eyes ehn...in fact I felt as if I was intruding."

Hope burst into helpless laughter at the ridiculous exaggeration. "I am not having this conversation with you girls. He was just being polite. I don't even know why you are all so crazy about him. I don't see what the big deal is. I'm going to my desk. I have work to do."

"Wait. Wait. Wait." Joy narrowed her eyes and peered at Hope. "So, you don't think he's hot?"

Hope shrugged. "He's okay."

"Hmm." Joy smirked. "He is the complete package o! There is nothing wrong with him."

Agnes nodded in fervent agreement and they launched into a conversation that started with "If someone like him asked me out ehn..."

Hope left them still discussing her non-existent flirting with Daniel Amadi and escaped into the main office. It was an open design, with glass walls on three sides, the partner's offices partitioned off at the rear, and one side taken over by a few enclosed conference rooms. In the main office space, multiple cubicles were arranged in open-ended squares, each square containing three workstations.

Hope made for her workstation, walking briskly, and stopping in her tracks when the doors to one of the conference rooms opened and two men emerged right onto her path.

She froze. For a moment, her heart seemed to stop, then it started pounding, hard and heavy against her chest. Her blood heated, too fast, giving her skin a weird sensation of flushing and freezing all at once. She wanted to keep walking, but her legs felt too weak, too shaky to carry the weight of her body.

One of the men was her direct supervisor. Greg Abudu, a friendly mechanical engineer and managing partner in his late thirties, who was just beginning to show early signs of a beer belly. He smiled widely, the way he always did whenever he saw Hope.

His companion was smiling too, eyes fixed on Hope's face with an expression of pleasant surprise.

Hope stared at the familiar face, her mind bubbling with emotion. How she hated that painfully handsome face! The pleasure in his brown eyes grated on her nerves as they slid over her face, silently declaring how glad he was to see her, how beautiful he thought it was that they had met again. She hated the illusion of friendliness and amiability that he projected. *I'm one of the good guys,* he seemed to say without speaking. *See how nice I am even though I am so handsome that I should be a demon. I'll never break your heart.*

But he had. He had broken her heart, in the worst way possible.

"Hope!" His voice was confident. She wished the sound was ugly to her ears, but it wasn't. No matter how much she hated him, she couldn't hate the sound of that velvety voice washing over her skin like a soft caress.

Hope didn't respond. She stood silent, causing Greg to start with awkward introductions, though it was obvious they knew each other.

"Charles this is Hope Alade, one of our building services engineers." He gave Hope a proud smile. "Hope, this is my friend Charles DaSilva. He's a manager at Bond bank."

"I know Hope well," Charles said smoothly, still smiling. He stepped closer to Hope. "Long time no see. Aren't you going to give me a hug at least?"

Of course not!

"Hello, Charles." She made no move toward him. He had taken too much from her to be entitled to anything else, even something as small as a hug.

"You look wonderful," he said softly. "More beautiful than I remember." His eyes did a leisurely journey over her face and figure. "I had no idea you worked here, or I'd have been around to see Greg sooner." He turned to Greg. "Hope and I know each other from way back in Uni. She was the love of my life," he said, turning back to face Hope with a smile on his perfect lips.

Hope stared at him, unable to staunch the bitterness and the anger. *One of the many loves of your life*, she thought. The memories were rushing back now. In those days, she'd tried to be careful. She hadn't been one of those girls who went wild at their first taste of freedom, whose sole purpose was to find a boyfriend and lose their unwanted innocence. She'd waited, determined to fall in love with someone special.

By her second year in school, all her friends were hooked up, some on their second or third boyfriends, but she continued to rebuff the guys who showed interest in her. It was easy, you only had to look at them, to hear them talk, to see that they only wanted one thing.

Then there was Charles. Unlike the childish boys she was used to, Charles was refreshing. He was a final year student, so good-looking it was impossible not to stare at him, but with a seeming unawareness of his cuteness that she couldn't help being drawn to him.

He was also the perfect gentleman, opening doors for strangers and always ready to help. In retrospect, Hope could see that all the strangers on the receiving end of his courtesy were pretty girls.

He was so gifted at making girls feel like queens, that it was almost too easy to fall in love with him.

She developed something close to obsession for him after a chance meeting at the library, where he helped her find the books she wanted and carried them to her reading desk, leaving her alone to read afterwards. Hardly able to concentrate, and unable to dispel the image of his perfect face for long enough to focus on the words on the pages, she'd been relieved when she was ready to leave, to find him waiting at the library car park.

"I wasn't waiting for you," he said, with a mischievous smile that made it obvious that he had.

That was the first day. After that, he always seemed to be there. He found out everything about her and he pursued her. She fell hard for him, but she couldn't bring herself to trust him. His interest in her came with the side effect of people she'd never even spoken to approaching her to warn her about him, and even though she shut down most of the gossip, she knew she had to be cautious.

He pursued her for a whole semester. Finally, it was the promise of sensuality and the entire world she could glimpse on the other side of his kisses that made her capitulate. Her body argued for him in a way that her brain was helpless to resist. First, she agreed to be a girlfriend, and soon, she was his lover.

She had been so happy and in love—the first time of falling in love is always like that. Free from the residue of past pain and heartbreak, it feels like the opening of a whole new universe.

It didn't take long to wake up to reality. While Charles had been waiting for her to say yes, he had been sleeping with someone else, someone who, as she discovered just a few weeks into their relationship, he was still seeing.

When she confronted him, he didn't bother to deny it. "How long was I supposed to wait?" he'd asked, his incredulous expression almost convincing her she was the ridiculous one. "I'm not built to be celibate. No man is, regardless of what you read in romance novels."

"But you're still sleeping with her," she'd wailed, desperate from a passion, possessiveness and jealousy that just weeks before, she wouldn't have known she was capable of feeling.

"I can't just tell her I'm no longer interested," Charles had replied. "Think about her feelings."

He made it sound like common-sense, like she would understand if only she were more mature. Still, she'd stormed out, spent the night crying in the hostel while her roommates exchanged knowing looks. Everybody knew about Charles DaSilva, and they'd all warned her.

But the next day he came to find her and said all the words she wanted to hear, promises of how she was the only one he wanted. There would be no one else from now on, he promised, and foolishly, she believed him, spending the next few years closing her eyes to all the evidence of his cheating, because she didn't want to feel the pain of losing him again.

But she still lost him. Right under her nose, he'd met, courted and gotten engaged to someone else. She'd graduated then, and was working at her first job, while waiting expectantly for the ring she'd deluded herself into thinking he would give her.

He hadn't even bothered to give her the dignity of ending their relationship properly, he'd allowed her to hear of his engagement through a mutual friend.

Keeping herself from confronting him was the hardest thing she'd ever done. She'd ignored his calls and finally changed her number. She instructed the security men and receptionists at her office never to let him in to see her. She refused to allow herself the temptation to listen to whatever explanation he would give.

He got married, about a year after she found out about the engagement. The transition from deluded girlfriend to bitter ex had been painful, but she dealt with the pain and the shame, and even though it took a while, she got her happiness and her confidence back.

She was still staring at him, Hope realised, coming back to the present.

Silently, she chided herself for behaving stupidly. When you met an ex-boyfriend again, you wanted to be beautiful, rich, and charming. To be enjoying your life visibly, and to show him in every gesture, word and smile, that you didn't care about him anymore, and that he had lost the world when he lost you.

So why was she acting like a churlish wife whose cheating husband had come back home to beg for forgiveness?

She smiled brightly, right into his face. "That was a long time ago, Charles," she said in a light, dismissive voice. She turned to Greg. "At that age, everybody fell in and out of love all the time."

Greg laughed. "I can attest to that!"

"I can't." Charles said earnestly, his eyes boring into hers. "My feelings were always very concrete, even then."

Even though she knew it was rubbish, Hope felt her heart squeeze. That look! She took a deep breath. "I hope you had a good meeting. It was nice to see you again Charles," she added, not meaning it at all.

He smiled back. "Seeing you has made my day."

She nodded and kept the smile on her face she stepped around them and took the few remaining steps to her desk, feeling his eyes on her back as she walked. She sat and turned on her system with shaking fingers, keeping her eyes fixed on her screen till the men were long gone.

CHAPTER THREE

GREG ABUDU's baby dedication was a couple of weeks later, on a Sunday. After a church service, which Hope hadn't been able to attend, there was a party at Greg's home.

Hope could hear the party as she drove into the estate where Greg's family lived, a serene and well-maintained compound with about ten large homes, a shared swimming pool, tennis courts, and carefully tended lawns. It was the sort of place you went to live when your hustling paid off and you finally *arrived*.

Hope parked close to Greg's house, a two-storey white and cream structure with huge classical columns. In the front lawn, there were canopies set up over lawn tables and chairs. A sweaty guy in one corner bent over a charcoal stove as he diligently prepared asun, the spicy, peppered goat meat dish that always made Hope weak in the knees. Next to him, was a huge table mounted with covered tableware out of which busy servers dished rice, soup, stews, and meats, before placing the heaped plates on trays to serve the guests.

Some guests were dancing, and many more were seated beneath the canopies. The band was playing one of the new local songs with beats that entered your brain, hooked into the tissue like pinworms, made you sing along even though you hated the lyrics, and made you dance even though you had no idea what the singers were talking about.

"Hope!" It was Greg's wife Mimi. Hope had met her a few times. She was a petite, stylish woman, and as she hurried to greet Hope, dressed in a well-made Woodin ensemble, there was none of the infirmity you would expect from someone who gave birth less than a month before. "Why are you just coming?" she scolded. "The party is almost over."

"I'm sorry." Hope returned Mimi's hug. "I hope I'm not too late."

Mimi shook her head. "Not really. In any case, the person we are all dancing for has slept off. Thank God."

Hope laughed. "These days we mostly get to dance at parties where the celebrants are sleeping."

"Exactly." Mimi took her arm. "Come and greet your boss," she said. "Then I'll find someone to serve you, okay?"

Hope nodded, allowing Mimi to lead her towards Greg, who was rocking the sleeping baby.

"Engineer!" Greg said, holding the baby carefully, as if any wrong move would spoil something irreplaceable. "How now?"

Hope replied with a smile. "I'm fine o." She peered at the baby's peaceful face. "Wow, he looks so much like you already."

Greg beamed with pride while Mimi rolled her eyes. "The next one will get my looks," she declared.

Greg laughed. "I was just about to take this small boss upstairs so he can sleep without any distraction. I think the music might be affecting him."

"Can he hear yet?" Hope asked, curious. The baby didn't seem at all concerned about the noise as he slept.

"They start hearing in the womb," Mimi told her, amused. "But I think Christopher likes music. Look how peaceful he is." She touched her baby's face, cooing softly.

"Awww." Hope smiled. "I love that name."

Mimi tugged at her arm. "Come and sit, so I can find someone to bring food for you." She led Hope to an empty table, leaving her with a promise to send a server her way.

Agnes waved at Hope from two tables away. She looked fantastic, her makeup and jewellery slightly more dramatic than her everyday office style, and she seemed to be having fun. Hope would have joined her, but the other table was full, and judging from the number of good-looking guys clustered around Agnes, there was no way she would leave that table to join Hope.

A server brought some wine and a glass, staying to open the bottle and pour out the wine. "Thank you," Hope said, letting her eyes wander around. There was something wrong in sitting alone at a party full of people you knew, she thought, slightly amused.

"Hope."

She froze, the glass of wine halfway to her lips. Charles had appeared in front of her, tall and handsome in a black embroidered caftan, and almost tortuous to look at. His expression was tender as he looked her over.

"Charles." Hope said his name dryly, hoping that the tone of her voice and the way she pursed her lips would be enough to make him leave her alone.

He chuckled. "Do you mind?" he asked, pulling

out a chair and joining her without waiting for an answer.

Of course she minded. She didn't want him anywhere near her. But she wasn't going to give him the satisfaction of thinking his presence had any effect on her. She let her eyes wash over him with pronounced disinterest, then sipped her wine quietly, ignoring him.

It had been almost two weeks since that day at her office, and she had since convinced herself that the chance encounter would not repeat itself. Now here he was, smiling at her and giving her that earnest look, as if he hadn't ripped out her heart and torn it to pieces.

Bastard.

What did he want anyway? For a weak moment, she allowed herself to fantasise about him throwing himself at her feet and begging for forgiveness. She had long ago composed the scornful words she would throw back at him, to hurt him the way he'd hurt her.

Biting back a sigh, Hope stole a glance at him and found his eyes fixed on her, a thoughtful look in their brown depths.

"I wasn't sure you'd be here, but I'm glad you came. I've been trying to get your number from Greg since last week you know, but he keeps posting me."

That was news to her, but Hope hid her surprise.

"Maybe he guessed that I don't want you to have it," she said. "Why would you ask him, anyway? He's my boss. He has no business handing my number to random ex-boyfriends."

"Random ex-boyfriends?" Charles's eyebrows went up. "We were together for five years, Hope. I'm not a random ex."

Hope laughed. It was a rude, scornful sound. Then she took a long sip of her wine and gave him a look that she hoped conveyed how little she cared what he thought.

His smile had faded. "There's no need to be hostile." He leaned closer and lowered his voice so it was barely above a whisper. "I should be given the chance to make amends, shouldn't I? To show you how much I have changed from the selfish and immature person I used to be?"

Hope stiffened. Why was he leaning in so close and whispering in that voice that made her think of things they had shared? Things like pleasure, intimacy... She frowned, angry with herself for remembering. He was still looking at her, his gaze intense, a half smile on his perfect face.

This is probably a game to him.

"I don't think it's necessary for you to show me anything," Hope said, setting her glass down on the table. Her hand was shaking slightly, and she quickly brought it to her lap, hiding it from his gaze. "I don't care if you've changed or not. I'm not holding any grudges." She got up, smiling wryly. "Now you can go and find another former girlfriend to placate. I'm sure we are many."

Charles's expression didn't change, and his eyes didn't leave her face. Hope turned away, forgetting to stay collected as she walked away from the table. In her haste, she walked into Daniel Amadi.

She almost lost her balance as she crashed into his tall, hard-bodied figure. Strong arms shot out to steady her, holding her against his solid chest for a short moment before he released her.

Hope stepped back, embarrassed. She tried to compose herself. In that moment, when she'd been flush against him, she'd felt the strong muscles of his masculine body, inhaled the cool scent of his cologne, the clean smell of his clothes. A crazy thought ran through her head about how much she would like for him to hold her again, and she pushed it away like a hot coal.

He's not even your type, she reminded herself. *You're just confused and flustered because of Charles.*

He looked good in a light-grey tailored shirt tucked into slim black pants. Broad shoulders filled out his shirt, and his clothes sat perfectly on him, showing off strong lean muscle. He looked casual, and yet somehow powerful. She remembered him in the lift, holding her purse out to her. There had been something strangely intimate in that moment, as if, for those few seconds the whole world had disappeared and it was just the two of them.

"Are you okay?" he asked, with a concerned frown. She'd never noticed how dark his eyes were. They were almost solid black, and intense, ringed with the long curling lashes she'd noticed before.

"Hope?"

She realised she was staring at him like a hypnotised rabbit. "I..." She cleared her throat. *Hope, focus. Focus.* "I'm fine. I just... I wasn't looking where I was going."

"Yes, I noticed," Daniel said, then smiled down at her.

Hope felt her breath escape her lungs, leaving her feeling slightly lightheaded. This was the second time she had seen him smile in the space of a few days, and there really was something about his smile. It made her question her conviction that he wasn't her type, and to wonder if she really had a type at all.

"I didn't expect to see you here," she said, her voice suddenly light and breathy.

"Really?" He chuckled. "Who can resist a baby's party?" he said wryly. "All of us grown-ups dressing up to celebrate for someone who has no idea what's going on."

Hope laughed. "I was just thinking the same thing."

Daniel raised an eyebrow. "Like minds, hmm?"

She may have imagined it, but it seemed like there was definitely something flirtatious in the way he said the words, in the look in his eyes and the tone of his voice. She felt her insides suffuse with warmth, and she realised that she was staring at him again, her lips parted softly as she pulled in a slow breath. She swallowed. Then wet her lips, suddenly nervous. *Focus. Focus. Focus.*

Daniel was still looking at her, in a way that made it difficult for Hope to think at all, much less speak.

"I... um... It was very nice to run into you here," she said.

He chuckled and pushed his hands into the pockets of his trousers. "It was um, very nice to run into you too."

"Okay," Hope breathed, turning around before she made a fool of herself. She made her escape, going over to the table where Agnes was basking in male attention. One seat had been vacated, so Hope stayed there for the rest of the party, talking about work and enjoying the food. She tried not to notice when Daniel left sometime later, walking to his car with Greg in tow.

The two men talked for a short while before Daniel drove off. Hope watched his car disappear from view, before turning her attention back to her companions. A few weeks ago, she'd never have thought Daniel Amadi would occupy her thoughts, but now...

Looking up, she noticed that a few tables away, Charles was now engaged in what seemed like a very flirtatious conversation with some girl Hope didn't know.

Where was his wife anyway? Why was he all over the place, alone, probably being a nuisance to unsuspecting young women? He caught her staring and gave her a slow, knowing smile. Hope looked away.

Later, after many other guests had left, Hope said goodbye to the proud parents and walked out to her car alone.

It was already past sunset, and even with the bright streetlamps in the estate, somewhat dark. She opened one of the rear car doors and bent over to place the party favour Mimi had given her–cakes, small chops and fried meats–on the back seat. As she straightened, her neck prickled in alarm, and she turned around, almost jumping out of her skin when she saw Charles standing behind her.

"I was admiring the view," he said, unapologetic. He unlocked a gleaming blue range rover parked next to her and carelessly placed his own party favour in the front passenger seat. "Did I tell you how good you look?" he murmured, turning back towards her. "You were always pretty, but now," he sighed. "I can't stop looking at you."

Hope swallowed, pain rising in her chest. She wanted to hurl insults at him, to say all the bitter things she had spent years imagining herself saying to him. She had built a future around this man, centred all her romantic dreams on him. He'd destroyed those dreams, and now he had the gall to tell her she looked good?

Calm down, a small voice whispered in her head. *He's not worth it.* "Don't say things like that to me," she told him.

"I can't help myself." He made no move to come towards her, but the apparent sincerity in his eyes was like a fist squeezing her chest. "Hope, I've never stopped thinking about you. You can't imagine how many times I've wondered what it would be like to see you again, and now I have, I'm completely blown away."

If someone asked her to describe how she felt in

that moment, Hope wouldn't have been able to. It was a mixture of emotions, resentment for him, because he'd broken her heart; regret, for all the dreams she'd lost when she lost him; and yearning, because no matter how much she blamed him, hated him even, there was a part of her, that had never left the past behind.

"I have to go," she said abruptly, climbing into her car. "Goodnight Charles."

She shut the door and watched as he came close to tap lightly on the glass. After a brief hesitation, she pressed the button to lower the window.

"What?"

"Can I call you at least?"

She chuckled bitterly. "No. There's no need."

"You're wrong."

"Maybe." Hope hit the button, and the glass started to go up. "But I don't care."

CHAPTER FOUR

THE NEXT WEEK was a busy one at the office. Hope and her team worked tirelessly to finish the engineering services drawings for a multi-storey office building in Lekki.

"Aren't you going to eat?" It was her mother, on Thursday night, hovering at the door to Hope's bedroom in their Gbagada home. Patience Alade was a tall woman, slim and beautiful for someone who was long past middle age. She watched, concerned, as Hope, still wearing her work clothes, collapsed across her bed in exhaustion.

"I'm not really hungry," Hope replied, kicking off her shoes. "I'm just tired." What she wanted was sleep. She'd been running around in the office all day juggling meetings with producing drawings. All that, combined with the drive home in bumper to bumper traffic, had left her so exhausted, she could barely lift her arms.

"We put your food in a cooler in the kitchen. At least try to eat something," her mother urged. "You can't keep working yourself like a machine. What if you were married? Would you come home like this—exhausted from work, unable to talk to or play with your children before going to bed."

Hope sighed, wondering once again why she still lived with her parents. If she was very prudent, she could afford to rent a mini-flat on the island like many of the older single girls she knew. She had toyed with the idea but had never gone through with it.

The main reason was...she had no interest in the stress that came with managing rent, Landlords, generators and all the stress that came with running a home. Without a social life or a serious relationship, she wasn't very desperate for privacy.

Her mother was still waiting for her to say something. "Well, I'm not married, mummy." Hope said patiently. "I'm single. I don't have children, and I'm exhausted. I told you we had a deadline at the office." She yawned. "I'll probably wake up later and eat. Tell Justina to leave the cooler on the kitchen counter."

"You don't have to do all the work in the office in one day, you know. You should learn where to stop to continue another day. You're too young to be living like this. No social life...just work, work, work. Your mates..."

Hope blocked out the rest of the speech. It was the same one she was familiar with. *"Your mates are married and are managing kids, family and careers..."* and so on and so forth. She closed her eyes and faked deep breathing, hoping her mother would go away. The faking became real after a while, because she woke up to her morning alarm.

She pulled herself out of bed, still tired. Her joints felt sore and achy. She was still wearing her work clothes from the day before, and as she stared at her reflection in the mirror over her dresser, she understood why her mother was so worried.

'Your mates are married and managing kids and careers.'

Well, she'd thought she'd be married by this time. In those heady days of her relationship with Charles. She'd hoped, prayed, believed that by the time she was twenty-seven she would have his rings on her finger and his child on her arm.

But life never worked out according to those plans...and who was to say there was anything wrong with her life as it was? She enjoyed her work. She even enjoyed the deadlines. That was more than most people could say and she was grateful for that.

She prepared for work quickly. She showered, dressed, applied her makeup, and went downstairs to make a sandwich and steal an apple from the fridge. It was still dark outside when she finished, and even Justina, their house-help was not yet awake. Hope noticed that there was no cooler on the counter. Her mother had rightly ignored her and probably put the food in the freezer. At least it wouldn't waste.

Outside, the gateman called out a greeting as she approached her car. "Aunty Hope. Good morning o."

"Good morning, Ayuba."

"Make I open gate now?"

Hope shook her head. "I'm not ready yet. I'll horn."

He went back inside his gatehouse. Hope tossed her bag into the car. In the driver's seat, she said a quick prayer before starting the engine. After a few minutes, she hit the horn and watched as Ayuba ran to open the gates.

"Hopefully," she muttered under her breath. "Today will be a good day."

———

IT WASN'T. Her car stopped in traffic, twice. And at

some point, even though she pressed down hard on the accelerator, it just kept slowing down. It took multiple times switching the engine off and on and a few curses from other motorists to get the car to the office.

It was Friday, and because her team had submitted their pressing deliverables the day before, it didn't seem like it would be a busy day. She attended a few meetings, checked and replied emails, and spent close to an hour on her daily crossword game. Soon, it was evening, and people started leaving. Her mechanic had come to the office in the morning to pick up the car, promising to return it in a few hours. At five in the evening, she was still waiting.

"Why not just take a cab home," Agnes suggested. She had redone her makeup and looked ready for an evening out with her date, some guy she'd just met. "Your mechanic can bring your car to your house tomorrow."

Hope shook her head, thinking of the gum-chewing mechanic with his grease-coated skinny jeans and eyes that filled with delight whenever her car got a fault. "That one will use my car for public transport. He'll do two trips to Ibadan before he returns it."

Agnes laughed. Her phone rang. "That's Bayo. I'm sure he's here. See you on Monday, love."

"Yeah. Have fun."

Hope waited thirty more minutes, then called the mechanic, who promised to have the car ready in another hour. Most of her colleagues had shut down their computers and left the office. She had nothing better to do than to idle on the internet. It was depressing, on a Friday night, to have nothing to do. No date, no nothing. Just an unreliable mechanic and a problematic car.

An hour later, she called the mechanic again. Another hour, he begged, detailing all the things he'd had to adjust or fix in the car. Hope cut the call and decided to check what movies were showing. Going to the galleria was an infinitely better option than waiting in the office until she was the only one keeping the security men from closing.

She found a movie she hadn't seen and took a cab over to the mall, buying a ticket and popcorn before going in to watch almost two hours of passable romantic comedy. The cynic in her couldn't help rolling her eyes at the happy ending and the whispered *awwws* from the audience in the dimly lit cinema.

Outside the theater, she checked her phone.

There were no missed calls, which meant that the mechanic hadn't finished with the car. She called him again and waited as the phone rang on his end. He didn't pick up. She tried again, and the number was switched off.

She cursed under her breath. Now, she had no choice but to take a cab. She stalked down the stairs, annoyed. The floor below the cinema entrances had several stores selling shoes, apparel, jewellery and more. She would have walked past them on her way towards the next set of stairs if she hadn't seen Charles emerging from one of them.

He was wearing a suit, dark grey, with a darker shirt beneath, and of course, he looked good enough to eat. He saw her and stopped, letting the door swing shut behind him as he assaulted her eyes with his perfection.

Hope wanted to keep walking. She wasn't in the mood to talk to him. She wondered if it would be rude if she just walked past. Probably. She slowed her pace, and he smiled, his eyes teasing.

"You look angry," he said, moving from the store entrance and coming to stand in her path. His gaze flicked past her to the crowd of moviegoers trickling down the stairs, then back to her. "Was the movie that bad?"

Hope shrugged. "No, not really." She gave him a thin smile, resisting the urge to ask what he was doing there. She didn't want to lengthen their encounter for any reason. "I'm on my way home," she said, starting to edge past him.

"Why the rush?" His eyes held hers, still smiling, still teasing. "It's Friday night. Nobody has to be home early on a Friday night."

She raised her eyebrows. "How about married people? With wives waiting for them?"

A sad half-smile played on his lips. "It's funny that I haven't seen you in years, and yet, in a month we've run into each other thrice."

Hope almost applauded at the deflection. "Funny is not the word I'd use."

"Really?"

She shrugged. "Irritating, maybe."

For some reason, he found her statement amusing. He laughed out loud, the sound familiar and full of memories.

"Look," Hope said, angry with herself for wanting to dive headfirst into those memories. "I have to go..."

"Are you driving?"

"No, I'm getting a cab," she replied, a second before realising that she had just given him an opening, one he didn't hesitate to take.

"I'll drop you," he stated, as if it was a done deal.

"No!" Hope scowled. "No." She had no intention of sharing a car with him all the way back to the mainland.

He looked surprised. "Why not?"

She chuckled, and even to her ears the sound was mirthless and bitter. "You are asking stupid questions," she snapped, walking past him.

He followed her downstairs. Outside, once they were past the burly security men at the entrance, he caught her hand.

"Hope."

She pulled her hand from his grasp. "What?"

He spared a quick glance at the people walking past them, the few eyes looking their way with thinly disguised interest. "I'm sorry, you know. I really am."

There was a torrent of tears threatening to burst from her eyes. "It's fine," she said with a shrug. "I moved on a long time ago."

Charles nodded. "I'd really like to take you home. I won't feel settled watching you get in one of these cabs. It might not be safe. Just let me, as an old friend."

You were never my friend. The words hovered on the tip of her tongue. A cab drove by, slowly, the hopeful driver unmindful of the cars honking behind him as he searched for a passenger.

"Come on," Charles said. He looked expectant, but with that same hint of sadness she'd seen in his eyes earlier. "You don't even have to talk to me if you don't want to."

Hope drew in a deep breath. "Okay," she said, resigned. "Where's your car?"

THE TRAFFIC on the bridge had reduced from peak levels, enough that instead of bumper to bumper traffic they could move at a steady crawl. Inside the cool air-conditioned interior of Charles's car, they were both silent, the only sound, the low hum of the engine and barely audible voices from the call-in program on the radio.

If it had been anybody else, Hope would have felt obliged to make conversation, but this was Charles, and she didn't owe him anything but resentment.

"So how long have you worked at Madueke and Makinde?" he asked, breaking the silence.

She snorted, her eyes going to his fingers on the wheel of the car. They were slim, graceful and tapered, with the nails neatly filed, buffed, and she noticed now, visibly missing a ring.

"Where's your wife?" she asked bluntly, ignoring his attempt at small talk.

He beat his fingers against the wheel in a series of light taps. "She left." His eyes skipped to hers and his lips lifted again in that sad half-smile from earlier. He turned back to the road. "So, you still live with your parents?"

She turned away from him, towards the window, still reeling from what he'd said. What did he mean *she left?* Was he no longer married? And if he wasn't... She closed her eyes as shame quickly followed the unbidden surge of hope.

He's the selfish bastard who broke your heart, Hope. Never forget that.

"You know how it is," she said calmly, pretending that he hadn't dropped a bombshell in her lap. "My parents are not the type to let me out without a ring on my finger."

His gaze flicked to her again. "That might happen sooner than they expect," he said quietly.

Hope frowned, the cynic in her convinced that he was dropping lines to tease her into letting down her guard, to make her think some part of their relationship was salvageable. Well, she would not fall into that trap. So, instead of responding, she concentrated her gaze on the view outside the car windows, the pale moonlight shimmering on the water. The giant billboard at the end of the bridge, everything but the man beside her, the man who'd once held her heart.

The silence stretched for a few more kilometres. He drove, and she refrained from asking about his marriage.

He didn't need directions to her parent's house. He'd been a regular guest back when they were still dating. He drove down the quiet street to park at the front of the gate.

"Thanks," Hope muttered, already reaching for the handle.

"Hope...wait."

She sighed. "What?"

"I know you have every reason to hate me, but I'm really sorry. I've spent years thinking about what I did to you. Every time I thought about coming to apologise to you face to face, but I was afraid that you'd hate me too much to listen..."

"Charles..." Hope exhaled a shaky breath. "Stop. There's no need for this. It was a long time ago. Like I said, I've moved on."

"So you've forgiven me?"

Hope shrugged. "Yes," she lied. "Forgiven and long forgotten."

He considered her for a couple of seconds, then leaned back on his seat. "So..." he gave her a lopsided grin. "Will you come with me to a party tomorrow evening? One of my friends is having a birthday soirée for his girlfriend."

"I don't... No." Hope shook her head. What was he doing? "I don't want to spend time with you."

"Why not?"

"Because..." Hope searched for words.

"Because you're still holding a grudge?"

She glared at him.

"If you haven't forgiven me, then we can use the opportunity to talk, and I can maybe explain. If you have forgiven me..." he shrugged. "It shouldn't be a big deal to attend a party with me."

Hope shook her head. "Maybe I don't feel like partying."

He chuckled. "Come on. If you've truly moved on, and we're just old friends at this point, there's no reason we can't hang out."

This was where she should ask him to clarify about his wife, Hope thought, but there was no way to ask without giving the impression that she was hoping for something more than just going to a party with him?

"Fine," she said, giving in. "Tomorrow when?"

"Around seven."

"Okay."

He grinned. "Okay."

She studied the triumphant expression on his face, before opening the door and sliding out of the car. Whatever it was she was doing, letting him close, flirting with whatever it was he was offering, she could only hope that she wouldn't end up regretting it.

CHAPTER FIVE

HOPE SPENT most of the next morning lounging in bed. It was almost noon when she finally got up and tidied her room, before taking a quick shower and going downstairs in search of something to eat.

Her father was in his favourite chair in the living room, with his glasses perched on the edge of his nose while he scowled suspiciously at the screen of his phone. He was in his sixties, newly retired, and happy to spend his retirement reading history books and biographies and giving information-rich lectures to anyone he could get to listen, usually his wife.

"Good morning, daddy."

"Good morning, madam." Madam had become his nickname for her from the day she got her first job. "I thought you'd already left for work."

"Daddy, today is Saturday."

"Oh." He laughed. "Retirement has caused me not to know the difference between the days of the week anymore."

"It can't be that bad."

"No. I like it," he replied. "I spent too long going to work every day. I'm glad to watch the days fade into each other."

Hope considered asking him what the problem was with the phone, but she decided to give him time to solve it on his own. It was probably something as simple as locating text message drafts. Older people liked to act as if the smallest issues they had with their phones were due to insubordination from the tech within the devices.

In the kitchen, Hope found her mother and Justina pouring bean paste for moinmoin into folded leaves, which her mother carefully set in a wide-bottomed pot for steaming.

"You finally woke up. I thought we wouldn't see you till tomorrow."

Hope chuckled. "Mummy, it's Saturday. After my hectic week, don't I deserve the rest?"

"Rest? Till afternoon? Okay. We'll be here when you have children. Shebi you will sleep when they're jumping on your bed crying for food."

Hope rolled her eyes. "If they have energy to jump, then they're not hungry." She ignored the frown on her mother's face. "Anyway mummy, you've forgotten that I used to do all this work Justina does now... I'm on housework parole. Time off for time served."

Her mother chuckled. "At least nobody can say I didn't train you well. I did my best. Are you hungry?"

"Dying," Hope replied.

"You're not dying in Jesus name," she muttered under her breath, prompting another eye roll from Hope and a muffled giggle from Justina.

"Aunty 'ope, Good morning," Justina chirped, her smile revealing the space where she'd lost a tooth before she came to live with them. She was fifteen years old. At least that was her best guess. She had been with them for four years now.

Hope remembered the big quarrel between her mother and her elder sister, Grace, when Justina first arrived. Grace felt very strongly about the fact that the girl was too young to be employed as a house girl. Her mother had dismissed Grace's concerns while taking them personally.

Hope had stayed out of it. It was a situation that could, and did lead to abuse in many homes, but she was more likely to make a difference in one girl's life at close proximity, than by enforcing ideals that would never touch the lives of the millions of disadvantaged children in the country.

Plus, Grace could always go home after her disagreements with their mum. Hope had no other home to go to.

"What's up, Jus Jus?" Hope said.

"I'm fine," Justina replied shyly. She practically beamed whenever Hope paid any attention to her. In her last year of junior secondary school and doing well academically, she'd confided that she wanted to be an engineer too, just like Hope.

"Have you guys had breakfast?" Hope asked.

"Your food is in the microwave," her mother said, placing the last of the moinmoin in the pot and watching as Justina put it on the cooker. "Yam and egg."

Hope went to retrieve the covered dish from the microwave. It was still warm, so she didn't bother to heat it. She set it on the kitchen counter and found a fork, coating a piece of yam with egg sauce before popping it in her mouth.

"Are you going to eat standing there...? Go to the dining... Justina! Why is the gas on the highest? When have we ever cooked moinmoin on the highest heat? You want to finish the gas? I have never seen a child that doesn't learn..."

Hope escaped the familiar tirade and went to sit in the adjoining dining room. She could see the TV as she ate, and her father had solved whatever the issue was with his phone and was now watching the news.

She didn't have to be anywhere until evening, when she would go with Charles to his friend's party. The thought made her apprehensive, and a little excited too. She wondered what her parents would say if they knew she had met Charles again, that she was letting him take her on what was in some ways, a date.

Her mother would flip, and her father would give her that disapproving look from beneath his glasses. She couldn't blame them. They'd been witness to the devastation Charles had caused when he broke her heart all those years ago, the spontaneous tears, the listlessness, the depression...

She wished there was someone to talk to, her sister maybe, but Grace would either be at the hospital or spending the morning with her family. Her younger brother Gerald was not the best person to consult about romantic stuff. He always pretended to listen for as long as he could bear before offering some unconnected solution, like a glass of Irish cream, a night at the club or a movie.

She would drive over to see one of them, Hope decided, before realising that she didn't have a car. The unreliable mechanic still hadn't called.

As the thought crossed her mind, her phone rang. It was the mechanic.

"Madam, sorry o! I swear as I dey repair your motor, I just sleep. I just sleep go. I no even know when I off my phone. Na so the sleep take catch me."

Hope snorted at the excuses. "Have you finished now?"

"Yes. I dey bring am come your office."

"Shebi you don't know today is Saturday? Why would I be in my office?"

"Sorry madam, I forget. I go bring am come your house. Just describe am. I go bring the motor come."

Hope considered trusting him with driving her car to the mainland, then decided against it. "Just take it to the office," she told him. "I'll come and pick it from there."

She finished breakfast and changed into jeans and a bright orange t-shirt with the slogan *the bigger the better,* then in smaller letters, *that's how I like my books.* She told her parents where she was going and listened to her mother go on about how mechanics on the mainland were more reliable. It wasn't true. In

Hope's experience, all car mechanics in Lagos, in fact the whole country, were the same.

She walked from her house to the estate gate. Thankfully, the sun was hiding behind a few benevolent clouds so she could add the few hundred steps to her fitness app without breaking a sweat. Outside the estate, she found an aging yellow cab with a grey-haired driver. They bartered and agreed on a price, and because the roads were free of traffic, in almost no time she was at her office.

A security man let her in through the front gate, and as she entered the building, she dialled the mechanic. Most of the offices were closed, but the building maintenance people provided the basics—generator power for when there was a power cut, water, security, etcetera—for the few companies that opened on the weekends.

"Sister, good afternoon o!" It was Alfred, the guy on duty at the ground floor reception, "but your people have not opened your office today."

Hope smiled at the young man. She liked him because he was always reading something, a book, newspaper or magazine, and she'd found out that he was pursuing a part-time degree. "We're not opening today. My mechanic is bringing my car here. I came to pick it up."

"Okay." He gestured at the waiting area in the

ground floor lobby, "You will wait here, or you want to go to the lobby on your floor?"

"I think I'll go up," Hope said. She'd brought her eBook reader, and she hoped to get some quality reading time in the quiet upstairs lobby in case the mechanic took his sweet time before showing up. She made her way to the elevator bank, stopping a few feet from the doors as one of them slid open to reveal Daniel Amadi.

He was looking down at his watch as he strode out of the lift, a striking figure in jeans and an unbuttoned short-sleeved shirt over a plain white t-shirt.

He was really hot, Hope admitted to herself, staring at the broad expanse of his chest, the tightly muscled arms...He was fit, athletic, but not overly bulky. She liked that.

Now, she couldn't remember why she'd ever thought he wasn't attractive.

He looked up from his watch, saw her standing there and stopped, a smile slowly spreading across his features. "Hope!"

She realised that she'd been staring and tried to cover up with a cheerful greeting. "Hi!"

"What are you doing here?" He frowned. "I didn't know you worked on Saturdays?"

"I usually don't, unless we have a crazy deadline...I...My car had a fault yesterday and the mechanic who fixed it is bringing it over here today, so I came to pick it up. I was just going to the lobby on my floor to wait." God! She was rambling like a nervous jambite straight from an all-girls boarding school.

Daniel looked slightly amused. His eyes went to the message on her t-shirt and his smile broadened. He raised an eyebrow. "Sooo...the car's been fixed?"

Hope nodded. "Yes."

"Good," Daniel said. "You won't have long to wait then."

"I hope so," she replied, wondering if, with the money he had, he ever had to deal with vehicle mechanics. He probably had a fleet of brand-new cars and changed each one as soon as the manufacturers made a new model.

"We were working on a technical problem with the servers. It's about fixed, though some of the engineers are still up there. I'm abandoning them." He smiled ruefully.

"The perks of being the boss," Hope teased.

He shrugged. "I wish. It's been a while since I slept. I've learned from experience that the efficacy of caffeine diminishes steadily the longer you stay awake. I'm so tired, even the floor of this lobby looks like a good place to crash right now."

Hope tried not to laugh at the image of him asleep on the lobby floor. She peered at his face. He did look tired. "You should go get some rest," she said. "Can't be crashing on lobby floors when you're the brains of the operation."

He smiled and started to walk away, then he stopped and turned back. "Hope?"

"Yes?" There was a wealth of expectation in her chest, causing a few stray butterflies to flutter senselessly in her tummy. It was silly, especially when she had no idea what he planned to say.

"What are you doing later, in the evening?"

"I...em..." She stopped, her excitement dissipating when she remembered Charles and the party she had already agreed to attend. "I'm hanging out with an old friend."

Daniel nodded slowly. "Okay." He shoved his hands into the pockets of his jeans. "See you around, then."

Hope watched him walk away, his tall, broad-shouldered figure moving with a graceful, loping stride. Would he have asked her to dinner, to hang out somewhere casual? Even without knowing him all that well, she felt like she had missed a chance to enjoy something good.

Her mind went to Charles, and she almost kicked herself. It made no sense that she had just turned down a date with a single and attractive guy like Daniel just so she could spend an evening with Charles, a married man who'd already shown her in the past how little she meant to him. It made no sense at all. It was the sort of thing that would make her mother clap her hands in dismay and question if Hope was really her daughter.

At that mental image of her mother, she chuckled and pressed the call button for the lift. She settled into one of the seats in the twelfth-floor lobby, and after spending a little more than an hour reading, her phone finally rang. It was the mechanic, calling to tell her he had delivered her car and was waiting downstairs.

HOPE SPENT the rest of the afternoon at her sister's place. Grace had returned from the hospital sometime in the morning and was now asleep. The children, bored with their nanny, welcomed Hope with boundless joy. They were two girls, six and four, and two boys, three and one.

Their father had just gone to the grocery store to do some shopping when Hope arrived, and the enthusiastic chorus of *Auntie Hope, Auntie Hope* was a sign of things to come. She spent the next few hours singing, drawing, watching cartoons, rocking the baby to sleep, helping with crosswords and rediscovering that children had an inexhaustible supply of energy.

By the time Grace woke up late in the afternoon, there was no time for the heart to heart that Hope wanted. She had to go back home to prepare for her evening with Charles.

Unlike during their relationship, when Charles would come into the house and sit with her parents in the living room discussing current affairs and career goals, this time he called her to let her know he was waiting outside.

"Who's this person you're going out with that cannot come inside and greet your parents?" her mother said when Hope came downstairs, all dressed up in a short peach dress, jewelled sandals, and light makeup.

"It's the first time we're going out. I don't think I want him meeting you guys and going through your interview when I don't even know if I like him yet."

"If you don't like him, why are you going out with him."

Hope looked to her father for help, but he

studiously ignored them both and fixed his eyes on the TV.

"It's just some guy I met in the office, mummy. No need for all this concern."

"Guy from the office and he can't come and greet your parents," Hope heard her mother mutter. It went on, but she'd already left the living room. She heard her father say something, and then her mother laughed. Hope chuckled. Now that she was out of earshot, they'd probably reminisce on how they used to sneak around on their own parents.

Outside, Charles was waiting in the car, running the engine and listening to nineties hip-hop.

"Hey," he drawled, his beautiful eyes doing a sensual journey from her face down to her legs. "You look good."

I look good but I wasn't good enough for you. The bitter words hovered on her lips and it took some effort not to say them out loud. "You don't look too bad," she said instead.

His smile was confident. He knew he looked good. Unbelievably good actually. There was something annoying and yet attractive about a guy who knew how good-looking he was and didn't hide it behind false modesty.

Guys who didn't seem to know that they were good-looking were also attractive, she thought, her mind going to Daniel Amadi. He had that aura, like he took care of himself but didn't measure himself by his appearance.

"So how was your day?" Charles asked, snapping her out of her thoughts. He lowered the volume of the music and smiled at her.

"Nothing much. I went to the office... Got my car back."

"Ah... your car! I forgot to ask. So, it's working okay now?"

"Yes."

Hope burned with questions. She wanted to ask him why he suddenly wanted to spend time with her, what the situation was with his marriage, why he threw appreciative glances her way every ten seconds as if he had a right to...but she stayed silent. Maybe after the party she would ask. For now, she would just take it moment by moment, enjoy his attention, toy with the desire to lash out at him the way she'd fantasised about doing for years.

Charles navigated the roads, leaving the estate behind as he headed for the island. "So...what's going on in your life?"

Hope shrugged.

"Come on," he cajoled. "Give me more than that. Is there a boyfriend?"

Hope barely swallowed the bitter snort that

threatened to come out of her mouth, smiling sweetly instead. "Not right now, no."

"Lagos guys are blind." He was smiling. "Look at you. Guys should be lining up at your door."

Hope was hovering somewhere between feeling flattered and confused. How did one respond when an ex said something like that?

"Who says they aren't?"

He grinned. "So, I have competition."

Hope was silent. Why would he say that?

"Charles."

"Hmm," he replied, his attention fixed on the road.

"What did you mean when you said your wife left?"

There was a long pause. "Why don't we talk about that later," he said finally.

There had been no traffic going to the island, so in no time, he swung into the parking lot of a new and popular café in Lekki. Inside, they had booked the whole mezzanine floor for the party.

The host was Frank Leton, a twice-divorced man in his late forties with interests in oil marketing and—according to gossip—419 activities. The girlfriend was at least twenty years younger and extraordinarily beautiful, just like the two women he'd already married and divorced.

He gave Hope a leering smile as Charles introduced them. The two men patted each other on the back, laughing at some joke she didn't understand.

She looked around, not sure what to think of the party. There were lots of girls, many younger than her, and the men were mostly older, late thirties, forties and fifties. Some of them wore wedding rings, though it was obvious that their companions were not their wives.

Hope sighed. It wasn't like she could judge, not when she was also here with a married man whose relationship status she hadn't confirmed.

Charles found them a table and ordered drinks. The place was flowing with drinks and food— expensive drinks, barbecued chicken, chips, peppered snails, goat meat, suya...Hope picked at the platter Charles set in front of her, enjoying each morsel.

Looking up at Charles, she found him watching her, a peculiar expression on his face.

"What?"

"Nothing," he smiled gently but kept his eyes on her face. "I've just missed looking at you."

Hope swallowed. Inside, an old ache came back to life. *You would have had years to look your fill if you hadn't chosen to dump me like yesterday's news.*

"Imagine that," she said, her voice dry.

Charles's expression was earnest. "You don't believe me?"

"It doesn't matter what I believe."

He reached for her hand and his fingers closed over hers. The contact was sweet and painful at the same time.

"It matters to me."

Hope closed her eyes.

"I love your hair," she heard him say, moments before he lifted his fingers to touch the strands in a light, casual stroke.

Hope sucked in a breath and moved slightly, creating a little distance between them.

Charles chuckled at her retreat, then leaned close. "You can't run away forever."

Hope pretended not to hear. She concentrated on the DJ, who was doing a very good job, and tried to ignore the man beside her to whom, she was finding out, she was still very much attracted.

"Do you want to dance?" Charles asked. "You were always such a good dancer."

Hope met his gaze, unnerved by the stark sexual appreciation she found there, unnerved by the way it made her feel. Pleased, flattered, flirty, wanting...

"Come on," he urged. "Dance with me."

Her eyes slid past him to the girls who were

dancing around the low tables. They were dancing for the men, not with them. Pretty little things gyrating and teasing and trying to keep the men's attention.

She realised what she'd felt before that she hadn't been able to put a finger on. It was a man's party, for men. The real guests were the men, and all the women were there as arm candy, to be looked at or lusted after. It wasn't her kind of party, and the whole thing felt sordid somehow, and it made her feel sordid to be there.

"I'm not getting up to dance for you," she told Charles. "What happened to *hanging out* as old friends?"

He laughed softly. "As you said, we were never friends."

"No," Hope agreed. "You're just some guy who abused my trust and was needlessly cruel to me."

Something crossed his face, a small expression of impatience, but he quickly replaced it with a smile. He leaned closer to her so that even with the thick aroma of alcohol, food and cigars, she could smell the freshness of his cologne. His fingers found her arm and stroked lightly, and though she wanted to be angry with him, she trembled with a faint and familiar hint of pleasure.

"One day," he whispered. "You'll forgive me, really forgive me. You know that, right?"

Hope forced a chuckle. "Is that a threat?"

"No, it's a fact." He grinned confidently. "And you know how I know? Because you never stopped loving me."

Hope wanted to laugh, to throw her platter of peppery dishes in his face, to push past him and walk out of the party, but she did none of those things.

He held her gaze, and her laughter died in her throat, as did the sharp retort on the tip of her tongue. Just from looking at him, she realised that he still had the power to reach her insides, to make her confused, to doubt herself, and to want him to be hers the way he had never truly been.

She forced a careless smile to hide the tumult she felt inside, laying her fingers on his cheek and stroking lightly.

"You think too much of yourself, Charles. You have to work on that."

He chuckled. To any onlooker, they would have looked very intimate. Hope didn't really care, because she didn't know anyone at the party. At least she thought so, until something made her look towards the stairs and she saw Daniel Amadi standing at the entrance to the mezzanine floor, his eyes locked on her.

Hope pulled her hand from Charles's cheek, mortified at what she assumed would be going through Daniel's mind. It was too late, Daniel smiled in her direction, nodded in greeting, then turned away—and in the short minutes he spent at the party, greeting the host and a few other people, he didn't look her way again, not even once.

CHAPTER SIX

After Daniel left the party, Hope lost the ability to enjoy the music, the food, or even Charles's dangerous flirtation, and deep down, she knew it was because of that look, that expression she'd seen on Daniel's face.

It wasn't judgement, or condemnation. It had been disappointment, followed by indifference.

Why? why? why?

From his point of view, it would have looked like she and Charles were lovers, and that she'd lied to him earlier about spending the evening with an old friend. Combined with the general tone of the party, which he'd obviously been unable to bear for more than a few minutes, his opinion of her had likely plummeted to subterranean depths.

"Are you all here?" Charles asked her. He was pouting. "You look preoccupied."

"I don't really feel..." Hope sighed. "I'm sorry, Charles, but I need to leave."

"Now?" He looked nonplussed. "But the party is just starting, and I hoped that after, we'd spend some more time together, you know, and..." he smiled. "...catch up."

Hope stared at him, then rose to her feet. "You don't have to come with me, you know. I know my way home."

He turned away, his eyes going to the girls dancing close to their table, and for a moment, Hope thought maybe he would let her go, and proceed to enjoy the rest of the night with one or two of the babes that were so plentiful, in which case, she'd need no other proof that he was still a piece of trash.

After a moment, he got up and held out a hand to her. "Fine, let's go."

He said his goodbyes to the host and led Hope out to where he'd parked his car.

"Was it the party? Do you want to go somewhere else?" he asked as he unlocked the car.

Hope shook her head. "No. Take me home."

His face soured.

"Look...I can request a cab if you'd rather..."

"Yeah, another thing for you to hate me for." He sighed. "Get in, Hope. I'll take you home."

Inside the car, Hope was quiet, ignoring Charles completely. In her mind, she saw that look on Daniel's face again and again, and it made her feel paralysed with embarrassment.

Why do I care so much about what he thinks?

The question played over and over in her mind as Charles drove. Daniel had no right to judge her. He didn't even know her. They'd only had a few short conversations. There was absolutely no reason for her to concern herself about what he thought, especially if he was a self-righteous and judgmental sort of person.

"What's the problem?" Charles asked, his voice cutting into her thoughts. "Did I say or do something to annoy you in there?"

"No, you didn't," Hope sighed. "I just wasn't enjoying myself anymore."

"That doesn't make me feel better," Charles said, his eyes skipping from the road to her face. "You might as well tell me you don't enjoy being around me."

Hope remembered the sexual tension of the moments before Daniel Amadi arrived and smiled. "I wouldn't exactly say that."

"But still you couldn't wait to leave."

Hope didn't reply.

There was a spot of traffic, and Charles studied her face, turning back to the road once the traffic cleared. "Did I come on too strong, is that it?"

"Charles..."

"You can tell me," he continued, interrupting her. "I've never stopped wanting you, Hope. And I won't lie and act as if I'm not crazy about you right now. I am. So...if it's too much...if you don't want to be around me at all...if you want me to disappear and leave you alone, just tell me."

Hope swallowed. If she said that was what she wanted, she'd be lying. She was still attracted to him. There was still something about him that drew her and made her want to risk...her common-sense...for the gratification of knowing that he still wanted to be with her, that he still found her attractive, that he regretted walking away from her.

Don't be a fool, she warned herself. She knew from experience that men like Charles could say anything, pretend for as long as it took to conquer a girl's defences. That was just the way they were wired. To see women as conquests, as victory stories to tell their friends over drinks.

She stole a glance at him. He was waiting for her answer, silent, his gaze on the road. What if she was wrong? What if he was hurting? What if he was lonely and missed her? She remembered that day at the office with Greg. He'd said that she was the love of his life.

She turned to the window, casting her gaze outside, and the silence stretched until Charles parked the car in front of the black-painted iron gates of her house.

He drummed his fingers on the wheel for what seemed like a long time before turning to her. "You didn't answer my question," he said, his voice quiet.

"You haven't told me what happened with your wife," Hope countered.

He let out a long breath, and Hope could have sworn she saw moisture in his eyes before he turned away.

"Many girls these days just want to get married," he said slowly. "It's a rite of passage. Something all their friends are doing." He sounded bitter, pained even. "A man is like an accessory to them. Someone to show off to their friends at parties while looking down on the unfortunate ones who haven't hooked one of their own."

It was the most sombre Hope had ever seen him. She looked down at her fingers, tempted to reach for him, to offer some words of comfort, but she held herself back with tremendous effort. He didn't deserve her pity or consideration. After all, it was he who'd made her a certified member of the group of *unfortunate ones*.

"Are you saying your wife...is like that?"

The car engine hummed low. Outside the car, the evening breeze ruffled the leaves of a solitary almond tree near a tall fence. Hope waited for Charles to respond. He didn't.

"Weren't you aware, before the wedding?" She prompted. "Why did you go along with it?" Internally, she was screaming. *I loved you with my whole being, and you chose to spend your life with someone who saw you as a prop with which to impress her friends?*

"I don't know that I was really aware. Maybe I was and instead told myself that she was in love with me. There was some family pressure too. Her family and mine are close, and once I'd been out with her a few times, they expected an engagement. You know how these things go."

She knew. Two families consolidating their relationship, pushing a beautiful young couple together to produce the next generation and increase the combined wealth and connections, especially considering that his wife's family had *a lot* of wealth and connections.

Hope studied his face, taking in the set of his jaw and his expression that, even in profile, communicated an intense mixture of anger and sadness at the same time.

"I always enjoyed being with you, you know. Even just talking. You were never boring. I was never lonely with you. You knew me, and you loved me for who I was."

Hope turned away, angry with him for even talking about their past relationship. He was the one who had thrown it away. Was she supposed to pity him now? He'd made his bed. It was his own fault that he was miserable.

"I'm sorry, Charles, but I don't know what you want me to do... How you want me to react to this? Are you saying your marriage is over? Am I supposed to be glad it failed, that you're free to take me to parties now?"

He shrugged. "I'm not asking you to do anything. She left and yes...it's given me a chance to spend time with you. I don't regret that."

"So, you're not planning to get her back? To work on your relationship at all?" She searched his eyes, not sure what she was looking for, what she was hoping. For a long time, bitter from his rejection, she'd hoped his marriage would fail. She'd dreamed of when he would come back crawling on his knees, of how she would punish him before forgiving him.

She'd never spared a thought for his wife, except

as the woman who'd stolen him from her. Her fantasies never considered the other woman's pain, and now, because of what he was saying, it felt like she'd been right not to.

Charles smiled sadly. "Why should I try to get her back? Seeing you again, Hope..." he sighed and took her hand in his, stroking her fingers. "I want you. I feel like I missed my chance to be happy before and I have it again...with you."

The words sent a tremor through her, the words, and the sensual warmth of his hand on hers. She swallowed as long-ago memories of pleasure unfurled like petals in her mind.

"I have to go inside." Her voice sounded strange even to her ears. She drew her hand from his. "Goodnight, Charles."

"Hope..."

She didn't reply. Almost clumsily, she pushed the car door open and stepped out, hurrying towards the closed gate. Her emotions were all over the place, and being with him, inside the confines of his car, with those memories from their shared past...it reawakened things in her body that she knew would be dangerous to explore.

Ayuba opened the gate with a toothy grin and Hope stepped inside the compound, quickly pushing the gate closed behind her, as if that barrier would somehow dam the feelings that were threatening to push her straight back into Charles' arms.

LATER THAT NIGHT, Hope tried to do some social media digging. She didn't know if Charles's wife had enough of a social profile for it to be a thing on the blogs if she left her husband, but she searched for her name on the local gossip blogs anyway.

Apart from the years old wedding spread, which had been on all the blogs there was no news of them. Hope checked all the popular social media sites, but it seemed like Charles's wife—or ex-wife—wasn't an active poster. There was nothing pointing towards a separation, but there was nothing pointing away from it either.

So, what if Charles was telling the truth? What if he was lonely and miserable and his marriage was over? Would she forgive him for the way he'd hurt her in the past just because there was now a chance to be with him again?

What if he hurt her again?

Was she a blind masochist for even considering giving him a chance?

She closed her eyes. She couldn't forget his voice, the words he'd said, the sincerity in his face when he told her he was lonely, that he missed her. *"I want you,"* he'd said, and the stark admission made her want to drop all her defences, all her anger and resentment, and pretend, just pretend that they were together again, the way they used to be.

You're a fool.

He broke your heart once, and he'll do it again.

Even when you were together, he was never really yours. He hurt you even then.

Stop romanticising the past.

Hope ignored all the voices, focusing instead of the feeling of being close to him again, the excitement she'd felt when he'd touched her, the tremors that had gone through her body.

She had a hard time going to sleep.

THE NEXT MONDAY, Hope listened to Agnes go on and on about her weekend. She'd spent almost the entire time with her new beau. "I think I'm in love with this one," she told Hope. "He's the full package."

"Is it him you like or his package?" Hope quipped.

Agnes laughed. "See your dirty mind. Later you'll say I'm the rotten one."

Hope wondered what Agnes would say if she told her about Charles, about the conflicting emotions barraging through her mind. She wanted desperately to talk to someone, but she didn't want anyone to make her feel foolish or careless for considering...

For considering what exactly? Going back to him? Having an affair? Dating him seriously?

It was all so impossibly ridiculous.

"How far you and Daniel Amadi now? I saw you two talking at Greg's baby dedication...Shey he hasn't made his move?"

Hope glanced quickly around the office, hoping no one had overheard. She remembered her encounter with Daniel during the weekend, and embarrassment surged again.

"I don't know what you're talking about," she told Agnes.

"Ok o, but if a guy like that showed even the least bit of interest in me..." The advice went on and on but after a few words, Hope tuned it out and went back to her thoughts.

What was really going on with Daniel, anyway? She didn't want to read anything into a few friendly words, and after the party on Saturday...well, judging from his expression, he'd probably formed an unflattering opinion about her.

She tried to ignore the pang of regret. There was just something about him, something that had hooked into her thoughts in the last few weeks and refused to let go, even when she was with Charles.

But she would not turn herself inside out trying to correct his assumptions, especially if he wanted to be unfairly judgemental.

At lunchtime, she had errands. She left her car in the office and walked through the paved Victoria island streets where converted residences housed all sorts of commercial enterprises, from office, to art galleries, to restaurants. She went first to the bank, then to a nearby store, before purchasing a snack at a local fast-food restaurant and heading back to the office. She entered the cool marble lobby and headed for the lifts, slowing her pace when she saw Daniel emerge.

He was wearing a magnificent three-piece suit that made him look fiercely handsome, like he just stepped out of a magazine spread about rich and successful entrepreneurs. Hope stared. Every time she saw him, he looked even better than the last time.

She stood rooted as he approached. Oddly nervous. Her stomach tightened and her heart thudded against her ribs. It was...disorienting.

He was flanked by three other men, who listened

as he spoke in a clipped voice. As they neared her, Daniel looked up and met her eyes.

His eyes seemed to slam into hers. She drew in a breath. *This makes no sense*, she thought, almost panicked. She smiled uncertainly, then lifted one hand to wave in his direction.

His response, a small inclination of his head, was hardly perceptible, his eyes slid off her, barely showing any recognition, and he continued his journey with his companions to the sliding glass exit doors.

CHAPTER SEVEN

HE'D PRACTICALLY LOOKED through her!

On the drive home, Hope was still thinking about that crushing snub from Daniel. Who did he think he was? How dare he act all friendly then get all cold and impersonal because...because he'd seen her at a party?

What did he think he was? The party prefect?

She decided, over and over again to forget about him, but her mind kept on replaying the moment he'd looked through her as if he only barely noticed her presence.

Her parents discussed politics at dinner, while the evening news filtered into the dining room from the TV in the living room. Her father was going on with one of his lectures again, talking about the *coup of the five majors* and its implications, while her mother listened tolerantly.

When Hope tired of the history lesson, she said goodnight and went upstairs to her room to get ready for bed, trying and failing to keep Daniel's face from appearing in her mind's eye.

Just as she got into bed, her phone started to vibrate. She saw Charles' name on the screen and realised that she'd been so preoccupied with Daniel that she'd barely thought of him all day.

"Hi, angel," he said as soon as she answered the call, and the simple endearment took Hope back through her memories to another place, another time.

"Hello." Her voice was soft with an unplanned tenderness. "How are you?"

"So, so." He paused. "I was wondering what you're doing."

"I was just going to bed."

"Hmm." She could hear the mischief in his voice, so his next question didn't surprise her. "What are you wearing?"

She only paused a beat. "Something very sexy. Satin, lots of lace, very low cut, and very short."

There was a long silence. "You're killing me," Charles said finally, his voice low.

Hope grinned. "You started it."

She heard him take a deep breath. "Let's have

dinner tomorrow. Tell me when you finish at work and I'll come pick you up."

She should have hesitated at least, or even considered refusing, but she wanted to see him, and she didn't want to keep lying to herself about it.

"You don't have to pick me up. I'll meet you at whichever restaurant we choose."

"Where's the romance in that?" he complained. "Can't you leave your car at the office or something?"

Hope considered it. "I could, but I don't want to get to work the next day and find that the real owners have collected the brain box and tires."

"The real owners?" He laughed. "You guys don't have security? Anyway," he continued, "Why don't we do it like this—I'll come and pick you up tomorrow morning, so you can leave your car at home. That way we get to spend more time together."

Spend more time together. Hope sucked in a nervous breath. She was treading on dangerous ground and she knew it. Already, he seemed to assume that they were back on track and seeing each other. Meanwhile, she knew that was a risk she shouldn't take.

Yet she was encouraging him

Taking pleasure in his attention.

Loving it, in fact.

"Fine," she told him, "You have to be here before seven though, and I close from work at five, but I hardly ever leave before six. You can pick me up then."

She could almost hear his grin through the phone. "See you tomorrow," he said. "I'm looking forward to it."

Hope smiled. "Goodnight Charles."

"Goodnight love."

She thought about that final endearment for a long time before sleep finally took her.

THE NEXT MORNING, Charles arrived on time. At half-past six, he'd already sent a message to tell her he was parked outside. Hope hurriedly finished her makeup and checked that she looked good. She had chosen a grey dress with pearl buttons leading up from the swell of her breasts to a black mandarin collar. After one last look in the mirror, she hurried downstairs.

"You no carry your motor today?" Ayuba enquired curiously as Hope hurried towards the small gate, her heels clicking on the interlocking concrete tiles on the driveway.

She shook her head, ignoring the gateman's

perplexed expression. He ran ahead of her and unlocked the small gate, his face showing comprehension and interest as soon as he saw the car parked outside.

Hope ignored him, walking over to Charles's car and climbing into the passenger seat. The stereo was playing dancehall music, but soft, almost too low to hear anything but the beats. Charles looked up as she entered, and his welcoming grin made her heart tighten a little.

"Good morning."

"Good—You look...wow!" he exclaimed, leaning back and arching an eyebrow at her. "Do you usually look like this every morning or is this a special effort for me?"

"Shut up," Hope laughed. "Stop flattering yourself."

"What's wrong with making an effort to look good for me?" he said, shifting the car to drive. "Aren't I worth it?"

Hope smiled. "Seeing as you drove all this way to pick me up, yeah, maybe."

He looked at her, a tender smile playing on his lips. She smiled back at him, forgetting, for that one moment, everything else...the past, the memories, the pain...and focusing only on the intimacy and pleasure of being with him in that moment.

He dumped you, Hope. Have you forgotten? And he has a wife. Don't forget that either.

Hope pushed the warning voice to the back of her mind. She was determined to enjoy the attention, and she did. By the time he arrived at her office, she'd spent most of the drive laughing at his teasing, teasing him and thinking maybe, if there weren't any obstacles in their way, it wouldn't be so bad to be with him again.

"I THINK the best option is to channel the storm water outside the estate and create a new storm drain, which will link to the existing canal, as Hope suggested...Hope, why are you smiling?"

Hope blinked at one of the senior partners at Maduekwe and Makinde. He was frowning deeply at her from his position at the head of the conference table.

"I'm not smiling," Hope stammered, turning her attention back to the drainage options projected on the screen. She'd spent the better part of the morning preparing the slides for the presentation along with her team of junior engineers, and now, instead of remaining focused, she was daydreaming about Charles.

Charles.

The confident, easy way, he'd taken back control of their relationship, brushing all her resentment aside as if they were no more substantial than spiderwebs... She knew she ought not to trust him, but she so badly wanted to.

"That's also my preferred option," she continued. "A storm-water purification plant would take us out of our budget, and a storm-water storage reservoir just to feed the sprinklers is also not cost effective."

The meeting proceeded, with Hope determined not to let her thoughts carry her out of the room again. In such a male-dominated industry as construction, it was important to her to always communicate competence and efficiency. There were a few of the older architects and engineers who used any small slip to confirm their old-fashioned biases about women in engineering.

"Great presentation," Greg told her later.

"Thanks."

"Hope..." he paused, as if considering what he wanted to say. "You know what...never mind."

She watched him walk to his office, wondering what he had been planning to say. Probably something about the project. She went back to her desk and spent the rest of the day focused on work, and by closing time, the junior engineers were glad to escape her endless demands for blown-up printouts and the inevitable red ink mark-ups that followed.

"If we keep working like this every day, we'll have to go and help other firms finish their work o, just to have something to do."

Hope smiled at Agnes, who was packing up her stuff and getting ready to leave for the day. "If we worked like this every day, we'd all be dead."

Agnes laughed. "So, you know you were trying to kill all the engineers today."

Hope stuck out her tongue. "I was inspired."

"Please don't be inspired tomorrow. I'm begging. Let us rest."

"How's it going with your full package guy?" Hope asked, laughing.

"Bayo?" Agnes made a face. "He hasn't called me since, and he's not picking my calls."

Hope raised her brows in alarm. "How come?"

"See ehn...I don't want to think, or talk about these men," Agnes shrugged. "I've stopped calling him sef. I can't be the desperate one again." She stopped and sighed. "See you tomorrow. Let's beat all our deadlines this month."

Hope nodded. "That's the spirit."

After Agnes left, Hope spent a few moments staring at her screen. She wasn't the type to press and press for details especially when the other person wasn't eager to share the information. She knew Agnes never held back when she liked a guy. She didn't play games and ration affection. Some guys appreciated that, others didn't.

Easy come, easy go. She'd once heard a course mate use those words to describe a girl he hadn't had to chase for too long. It still annoyed her now, many years later.

Was it her place to advise Agnes to be less trusting of the men that approached her, to be more discerning, to try to confirm that they deserved her time before jumping into intimacy with them? She didn't know. It wasn't like her own love life was so much better.

She freshened her makeup and waited for Charles to call, using the time to catch up with an episode of her favourite sitcom. Her phone rang just when the end credits appeared on the screen.

"How's my sweetheart?" Charles said as soon as she picked up.

Her heart flipped. "Who's your sweetheart?" she replied, smiling, and trying to ignore the sweet ache in her chest.

Charles laughed. "I'm outside your office, babe. Are you ready for me?"

Babe.

"Ready for what? Is it not just food we're going to eat?"

There was amusement in his deep voice. "You never know."

Those words stayed in her mind as she left the office and took the lift down to the lobby.

You never know.

Like it was possible their night would end some other way?

At the thought, she felt her stomach knot. It would be so idiotic to let down all her defences and allow Charles back into her life, heart...and body.

And she was determined not to be idiotic.

Charles' car was idling just outside the gates, visible through the low fence. As she approached, he got out of the car and strode over to the passenger side to open the door.

He was wearing the same clothes from earlier, a tailored shirt, eggshell blue, with pearly white buttons, over dark pants that framed his long legs. He didn't hug her, and with the car door between them, she managed to restrain herself from throwing her body into his arms.

Nobody should look that good.

Certainly not an ex-boyfriend who could still make her heart race with just one smile.

Hope climbed into the car and filled her lungs with cooling air.

"I don't trust you," she said, once he joined her inside.

He paused in the motion of fastening his seatbelt. "Why on earth not?" he asked, eyes wide with exaggerated innocence.

Hope laughed. "Opening car doors? Come on, Charles! When did you start doing that?"

He chuckled and started to drive. "Sweetheart, why not just accept it like the princess you are?"

Hope laughed. "Nah. You're definitely fattening me up for the slaughter. You're the big bad wolf, and I should be careful."

Charles shrugged. "I don't mind that image. You know that story—red riding hood and the wolf—has a lot of erotic symbolism."

"No, it doesn't."

"Oh, it does. It's definitely about the wolf seducing red riding hood. *All the better to eat you with?*" he grinned slyly. "Come on, it's definitely about sex."

Hope bit her lip, unable to think of a reply. She should change the subject. Talking about sex with Charles would lead nowhere she wanted to go.

Anywhere she *should* go, at least not with him.

"Where are we going?"

"First a drink, then a long, satisfying dinner, so you can tell me all that's been happening since... these past years."

Since you dumped me, you mean. The unsaid words hung in the air, but if Charles felt them, he didn't let on. He concentrated on navigating the evening traffic, and asked about the project Hope was working on, seemingly interested as she described mechanical works and design restrictions.

He shared stories about his work in the bank, and how crazy it was. They were hilarious and peppered with names she'd only encountered before in newspapers. She tried not to be too impressed.

Drinks were at a lounge at the very edge of Victoria Island with dim lights and a private and intimate seating area where all sorts of things seemed possible.

Once seated, she looked over the cocktail list, deeply aware of Charles seated so close to her.

"You should order the screaming orgasm," he said, leaning close. "I've never met a woman who didn't like that one."

Why was it suddenly so hot inside the lounge? Hope resisted the urge to fan herself. "You're obviously an expert on women," she replied, not surprised at how breathy her voice sounded.

He smiled slyly. "I am."

She pulled in a breath and took his advice, ordering the cocktail and a seafood platter.

Hope tried to keep her eyes on the food as she ate. She focused on the plates, the other tables, anything but Charles. It was too hard to look at him, especially when his eyes never seemed to leave her face. In his gaze, there was a mixture of desire and reverence, coupled with the latent attraction that, she realised now, had never really gone away.

If she'd brought her car, she'd have found an excuse to leave. Maybe he knew that. Maybe he'd wanted her to have no readily available options to help her escape the intensity of *him*.

Hope concentrated on finishing the fried prawns on her plate, almost gulping her cocktail. "I feel like I could eat bags of that fried shrimp," she said with feigned lightness.

Charles smiled, his eyes still on her face. "Better not. You should leave space for dinner."

"And where is that happening?"

He shrugged. "You'll see."

By the time they left the lounge, the roads were free. Charles drove through Victoria Island and took the bridge into Ikoyi.

It wasn't until he stopped in front of a wide white gate that Hope first suspected that they might not be going to a restaurant as she'd thought. The gate slid open, and a uniformed security man waved a greeting at Charles as he drove in.

The brightly lit building was a modern block of large luxury apartments. Hope stayed silent as Charles parked, trying to unpack her feelings about going to his home.

There was a mild curiosity—she wanted to know where he lived, and yes, it would give her an opportunity to find out for sure that there was no significant other lurking somewhere. If it was a home he shared with a wife, there was no way there wouldn't be some sign.

There was also hesitation. Going into his home wasn't a figurative crossing of the Rubicon, regardless of how many people saw it that way, but it would open a door, a door to letting go of her doubts and hesitance, a door to giving Charles what he so obviously wanted.

What she wanted too.

Because there was no denying that she wanted him.

He switched off the engine and grinned in her direction. "All set?"

After a slight pause, Hope nodded. "Yes. Though I didn't know we were coming to your place."

A concerned look crossed his features. "I hope

you don't mind, but I have a very good cook. Trust me, his cooking is better than you'll find at ninety percent of the restaurants in Lagos."

"No problem," Hope climbed out of the car, swallowing her hesitation. Beyond the parking lot, the compound was beautifully landscaped, with walkways, hedges, flowers, colourful shrubs, and a few trees with leaves rustling gently in the cool night breeze. Charles took her hand and led her towards the entrance of the building.

He held on to that hand all the way through the lobby, into the lift and up to his apartment. All her senses focused on that touch until she could think about nothing else.

Inside his well-furnished apartment, she finally pulled her hand from his, causing him to raise an eyebrow in a silent question. She ignored him, concentrating on her surroundings, the tasteful art and décor, high ornamented ceilings, luxurious furniture, and skilfully done finishes.

"You have a beautiful home."

Charles waved dismissively. "Thanks. Would you like me to show you around, or would you like to eat first?"

The words *show you around* conjured images of him leading her through the apartment to his bedroom, and showing her, well, showing her things she'd long tried to forget. Hope cursed her imagination. "I think I should eat ASAP. I'm hungry again."

Charles laughed. "I remember your appetite. Let's eat then. Why don't you have a seat while I tell my cook to serve the food?"

"Okay." Hope settled into one of the plush settees just as a smallish man appeared from a doorway she assumed led to the kitchen. He greeted her effusively, and after Charles informed him they were ready for dinner, he disappeared and returned a few moments later to set the table.

Charles switched on the TV but turned it to some radio channel, so the sounds of mellow jazz filtered through hidden speakers. Then he joined Hope on the settee.

"I hope you're not pissed that I brought you here," he said.

Not pissed. Apprehensive, maybe, a little shaky, definitely excited... Hope shook her head, "Of course not. It's a great-looking place. At least now I know you don't live in a cave with skeletons all over the floor."

He guffawed loudly. "No. My skeletons are safe in my closet."

Hope studied him, not sure what to make of that statement. "Really? So...you have skeletons."

"Don't we all?"

Maybe, but there were different types of skeletons.

She didn't have the chance to say that, because just then, the cook reappeared and announced that dinner was served.

Charles rose from the settee and held one hand out towards her.

"Come on," he said, his voice teasing. "Let me fill you up."

Her eyes widened at the obvious double entendre, but Charles held her gaze, looking innocent. She let him lead her to the table, wondering what his skeletons were.

He broke your heart once. He's someone else's husband. What skeleton can be worse than all that?

She ignored the voice of common sense in her head and focused on the food, well-garnished seafood rice with salad and fried plantains served with a bottle of mellow red wine.

"You can't eat like this every day and not get hopelessly fat," Hope said after she'd eaten the last morsel of food. She took a sip of her wine and sighed. "I'm in heaven."

"I eat like this almost every day, but I work out a lot," Charles told her. "Gotta keep fit and strong, you know?"

"I'm sure. For the gyals dem." Hope spared a glance at his chest where the firm muscles were barely hidden by his shirt.

He laughed and refilled her glass before leading her back to the living room. They settled into one of the settees, side by side, so close that the scent of his spicy cologne filled Hope's nose, drawing her in like an insect to nectar.

She knew she should put some distance between them, but she didn't want to. He watched her drink her wine, and she held his gaze. He smiled at her and her skin flushed.

She read the intention in his eyes, the realisation of what the evening still had in store, but she couldn't say for sure if she wanted to leave or stay to experience the pleasure she knew she would find in his arms.

He stroked her arm with his fingertips, trailing a path on her skin and making her tremble, then he turned back to the TV and changed the channel to one where a rerun of a popular comedy sit-com was showing.

He was still stroking her arm as they watched the show. Hope laughed at the hilarious one-liners, sipped her wine, and felt her whole body relaxing into his touch. By the time the credits started to show on the screen, her head was resting on his shoulder.

He turned down the volume and turned to face her. So close, all she could see was how perfect he was, how she had missed everything about his face, his features...

"I've missed you so much," he whispered, taking her hand in his. "There's been no one else like you."

Maybe it was because his tone was so low, almost a whisper, or maybe it was the wine, but everything about him—the timbre of his voice, his expression—made him look so sincere, that Hope desperately wanted to believe every word that came out of his mouth.

"Charles..."

"Shhh." He leaned forward and with one hand leisurely stroking the back of her neck, brought her face closer to his. Their lips touched and Hope tried not to sigh with pleasure...and the satisfaction of experiencing that intimate contact again.

His lips covered hers, warm and firm and soft at the same time, and then his tongue was stroking her lower lip, then pushing at the seam of her lips, delving inside her mouth... His tongue touched hers and her eyelids fluttered. She moved closer, wanting more.

He deepened the kiss. He tasted of wine and smelled like heaven. His hands moved leisurely, over her shoulders, her back, down her sides, skimming the sides of her breasts, so slowly that she started to ache all over. Somehow, she was falling back on the settee, and he was covering her body with his, one of his hands found the hem of her dress and moved underneath it, skimming the trembling flesh of her thighs and moving higher, taking the dress up with it.

He broke the kiss long enough for his lips to trail along her chin towards her ear, his breath fanning her sensitive skin. Her hands were stroking his back, and there was a moan on the verge of escaping her lips. I want this, she thought. I want this so much.

Why shouldn't I have this?

Because it's Charles, her pleasure-soaked brain replied. You can't trust him. After the pleasure, there will be pain, because that's just how he is.

His lips were making their way to the base of her ear now, his tongue flicking out to find sensitive spots he knew from long ago, making her tremble in his arms. She moved her hands from his back to his chest and pushed gently. "Charles," she whispered.

"Hmm," he said without stopping. On her thigh, his hand slid higher.

She pushed a little more firmly, and his body stiffened. He faced her. "What's wrong?"

Hope tried to shift back, but his hands—on her thigh and back—had tightened considerably. She took a deep breath, trying not to look straight into his face. She was still trembling, still needy, one look at him and she might just let common sense go. "I think I should go home."

"No, you don't," he murmured. "You think you should stay." He leaned forward to kiss her again.

Hope stiffened and shifted back as far as she could. "Charles!" Her voice was sharp.

For a second, he looked very pissed. He released her and watched as she moved as far away from him as she could on the settee.

"Are you serious?" His voice was cold.

Hope bristled from the coldness in his voice. "Do I look like I'm joking?"

His eyes raked her, and she tried to imagine what he saw, the rumpled dress, the mussed hair...she probably looked like sex in a minute.

Hope stood and ran a hand through her hair. "I don't want to move this fast," she said in a conciliatory tone.

"Why? Because you don't trust me?"

She met his gaze. "Should I?"

His eyes skittered away from hers, a moment before he shrugged and faced her again. "Look... we're both adults. This isn't like back then when you were holding on to your precious hymen. We're not kids anymore. We can enjoy being together without overthinking it."

Hope blew out an exasperated breath. How could she not overthink it? He was the same guy who'd broken her heart and stolen her illusions. She didn't have any problem with two adults taking pleasure from each other, but she didn't want to be the adult thinking things could be serious while the other adult just wanted to get his rocks off and walk away. Again.

"I can't not overthink it." She closed her eyes. "You used to mean so much to me, Charles, and if I stay, you'll end up meaning as much to me again. And if you don't feel the same way, if you treat me the way you treated me before, it'll hurt all over again, even worse this time."

A part of her wanted him to assure her he would never hurt her again. She wanted to hear him make promises, give her assurances, give her reasons to make this mistake...but he didn't.

He got to his feet, looming over her as he straightened his shirt. "I don't know what you want me to say." His voice was hard, with none of the gentleness and charm of the past few days. "I've said that I never stopped thinking about you." He went to the table by the front door and picked up his car keys. "Let me take you home."

His tone annoyed her, the unspoken insinuation that she was the immature, unreasonable one. *Is it supposed to be enough that you 'never stopped thinking about me?* She wanted to yell. *Is that supposed to be enough for me to throw myself into your arms after all these years?*

Silent, she followed him out of the apartment.

They didn't talk on the drive to the mainland. In less than half an hour, he'd parked outside her house.

His body language told her he was disappointed, and it annoyed her he didn't even have the grace to hide it. It made her feel as if, to him, sex was the only reason they'd gone out in the first place.

She opened the car door. "Goodnight," she said throwing a quick glance in his direction.

She found him looking at her. His eyes stayed on her for a long moment, keeping her from leaving the car, then he turned his gaze away. "Goodnight, Hope."

She smiled ruefully as she climbed out of the car and closed the door. Immediately, Charles started to drive away, leaving her standing out there alone on the street.

She went to the gate, feeling a sort of sadness weighing over her. After a few seconds of knocking, Ayuba let her in, and as she walked towards the house, she wondered if that was that—the end of this particular episode of Charles's presence in her life.

CHAPTER EIGHT

Hope's phone rang while she was getting ready for work the next morning, and she was surprised to see Charles's name on the screen.

"Hello," she answered dully, wondering what he wanted after the disaster of the night before.

"I'm outside the gate," he told her.

"You're here?"

She heard him sigh. "Hope...I'm sorry about yesterday. I want to talk."

"Talk?" she repeated dumbly.

"Yes." There was a pause. "And maybe try again?"

Try again? Everything sensible inside her brain screamed for her to refuse. The silence stretched. She imagined him sitting outside in his car, waiting. She imagined telling him to get lost. She imagined his face as he drove off, that hint of sadness, the small sad smile...

"I'm surprised," Hope said slowly. "I wasn't expecting you to come all the way here."

"I understand." He paused. "Why don't we talk when you come down?"

She rushed through all her preparations so as not to keep him waiting for too long. Outside, Ayuba didn't bother to ask why she wasn't taking her car. He opened the small gate and watched silently as she went over to join Charles in his car.

As usual, mellow music was playing on the radio. Charles had one hand on the wheel, fingers tapping. His shirt was crispy white, and even with her unsettled feelings about their date the night before, she couldn't help the faint longing that seeped into her thoughts.

His eyes met hers, his expression unreadable. "Hi," he murmured.

"Hi," she replied in the same tone.

He started to drive, still quiet, leaving Hope wondering if he planned to say anything at all about what happened.

"I'm sorry about yesterday," he said after a while.

Hope studied his profile. What exactly was he sorry about? The near-sex experience in his apartment, or the way he'd acted like a sulky kid when he didn't get what he wanted.

"I've never stopped thinking about you." His voice was low. "And yesterday I got carried away. It's just...there's so much I want to have with you, Hope."

What about what I want? Hope thought. *I want to know I can trust you. I want to be sure that the past won't repeat itself.*

"I don't know, Charles," she whispered. "Whatever it is you want...you'll have to give it time."

At first, he didn't respond, then he nodded slightly. "Fair enough."

They were both silent as he navigated the traffic. Though the sky was only just lightening to early morning grey, the roads were already teeming with cars and buses ranging from luxurious to rickety, ferrying Lagosians to another workday.

"I'll pick you up at the same time in the evening...so we can do dinner again." Charles said.

Hope gave him a sidelong glance. He looked like he really wanted this, like he really cared about seeing her again.

"Okay, but at a restaurant, this time." Hope shrugged. "I'm not going back to your place, and you have to take me home immediately after dinner."

His face was a mixture of contemplation and

amusement, then he nodded acquiescence, and his eyes went back to the road.

They didn't talk much until they reached Hope's office. After he dropped her off, Hope watched him drive away, puzzled that he was still trying. Why? Could it be that he was sincere, that he really wanted to work towards something meaningful?

Well, time would tell. She would take it one day at a time and see where it went.

At the elevator bank, she spent a few seconds waiting for a lift, and when one of the doors slid open, she entered. She turned back to face the main lobby as the doors closed slowly, and saw Daniel Amadi walking towards her with his confident, unhurried stride.

Damn.

Her reaction was intense and disconcerting. Her heart kicked in her chest, making her dizzy. She'd tried not to think about him since he snubbed her the other day, and with Charles occupying most of her time, it had been possible to think less and less of him, until she convinced herself that he didn't really matter.

That conviction felt ridiculous now as he walked toward her. She held the lift for him, trembling a little, feeling a weird mixture of anticipation and something that felt almost like dread.

He joined her inside, his nearness making her feel as if there was something preventing her lungs from getting enough air, as if he'd suddenly sucked all the breathable air out of the small space. As the doors slid closed, he smiled at her.

"Hello, Hope."

She attempted a smile in response. She didn't understand her reaction to him. It wasn't anything like her reaction to Charles. With Charles, there was the nostalgia and longing from all the memories they shared, and of course some sexual attraction. With Daniel, it felt as if he invaded all her senses and somehow, without doing anything, could make her uncertain about what she wanted.

"Hi." She watched as he entered the number for his floor. Then his eyes fixed on her face, still with a hint of a smile. It was a big contrast to the way he'd looked at her at that god-forsaken party.

"You look great," he said, his tone pleasant. "How's work going?"

"Fine." Hope smiled up at him. Her voice was calm, unlike her chaotic thoughts and emotions. "And you? How are you?"

"Never better." His broad shoulders moved in a small shrug and Hope pulled in a sharp breath. His proximity was making her dizzy.

For a moment, he looked like he would say

something else, but the lift came to a stop, and the doors slid open. They were already on her floor. Hope moved towards the doors, strangely hesitant to leave him.

"Have a great day," she said.

One side of his mouth lifted in a crooked smile. "You too, Hope."

She felt breathless as she walked into the reception of her office. It was a perfectly innocuous exchange, so why was she so tense, so shaky, so...confused.

It was a slow day, but as the work piled up little by little, she stopped thinking about Daniel, or Charles. She sent off mechanical drawings to the head of the branch development department of a popular bank, and the head of the department sent them back almost immediately with enough questions and comments that she almost screamed with exasperation.

There was a meeting with the architects from their partner firm, and one of the senior architects who had once asked Hope out and was still stung by her rejection insisted on acting grumpy throughout.

It was just one of those days, and by close of business, Hope was relieved it was over. At five, when most people started to leave the office, she freshened her makeup and settled down to wait for

Charles, though she wasn't sure when exactly he was coming.

He called a few minutes into her wait.

"What's up?" she asked cheerfully.

"Nothing much." He sounded tired. "Still at work?"

She frowned. "Where else would I be? I'm waiting for you. We're still having dinner tonight, aren't we?"

"Of course," he said quickly. "Look, I have a meeting that's taking forever to end, so I'll run a little late."

Maybe we should cancel.

The words hovered on the tip of her tongue, but she didn't want it to seem like she was still salty about the night before.

"Call me when you're done with your meeting," she said instead.

"I will."

She spent the next few hours doing some more work, then catching up on her TV shows. It started to get dark outside, but Charles didn't call again.

After a while, Hope realised she was practically alone in the office. Almost everyone had left, with only two of the senior partners still inside their offices.

She freshened her makeup, and after waiting for

a few more minutes, went down to the main reception and lobby.

The lone security man at the inquiries desk waved at her over his newspaper wrapped fried yam and suya. She waved back, a little envious. The simple roadside meal beat waiting for Charles.

Settling on a chair in the waiting area, she fished her eBook reader out of her bag and started to read.

She woke up with a start some time later. Someone had switched off the lights, except for the lights over the reception desk, where the security man from earlier was trying not to nod off. She glanced at her watch. About an hour and a half had passed since she left her office. Panicking, she reached for her phone, expecting to see a torrent of missed calls from Charles, but she was shocked to find none.

Not even one call.

He'd kept her waiting this long, and he hadn't even bothered to call.

It was unbelievable.

But was it so surprising?

It was Charles after all. By now, the only constant was that he would surely disappoint her.

She rose and glanced around the empty lobby, then sighed and collapsed back down on the chair.

Her only choice now, was to call a cab, so she got her phone and started to do just that.

She heard the lift beep, and then footsteps as someone entered the lobby, but didn't pay much attention. The phone call for the cab was taking a long time to connect, and it was too late to go outside alone to try to flag down a taxi. The street was much too lonely at night.

The footsteps stopped, then Daniel Amadi's voice. "Hope?"

She turned around to see his tall frame near the reception desk, illuminated by the bright lights in that part of the room. He'd discarded his jacket from earlier in the day, and the sleeves of his shirt were rolled up to expose strong forearms. She spent a moment admiring him, allowing her body to indulge in its the primal response to his physicality.

He strode over to where she was, his expression puzzled and concerned. "What are you still doing here? It's very late. Is it a problem with your car again?"

She shook her head. "Nothing like that. I'm... I was waiting for someone, then I slept off."

He chuckled. "You must have been exhausted." He studied her face and sighed, then looked at his watch. "Are you going to keep waiting? They'll be closing the place for the day any time now."

"No, I'm not." Hope shook her head. She was embarrassed, sure he had guessed that she'd been waiting for a man. Was he now judging her for being the sort of girl men kept waiting, the sort of girl who accepted such behaviour without complaint because she thought it was all she deserved? "I was just calling a cab."

Daniel frowned. "I'll take you home," he stated, his voice decisive. "I wouldn't trust any cab with you so late at night."

There was something possessive about the way he said the words, and it made Hope's heart skip.

Get a grip, she told herself. *He's a man, like the one who just kept you waiting for no good reason.*

His eyes were still on her face, his gaze soft and gentle. "You don't mind if I take you, do you?"

Hope shook her head, taken aback by the momentary glimpse of uncertainty in his features. Why did he think she would mind? She was out of options, and he was saving her from the potential horrors of Lagos after dark. "It's fine," she told him. "I'm actually very grateful. Thanks."

He nodded. "I'll get the car. You can wait at the entrance." He watched as she picked up her things. "Have you had anything to eat? Dinner?"

Her stomach rumbled. "No."

There was a long pause. "Would you mind having dinner with me? I was just about to."

Would it be a date? Hope wondered, knowing that the thought was ridiculous. "I don't mind. I'm famished."

"Good." His eyes dug into hers, and she stared back, caught in that gaze, then he looked away. "I'll go get the car."

Hope waited for him in front of the entrance doors. In only a few moments, he drove up in a black SUV with darkly tinted windows. As she walked over to the passenger side, he leaned over and opened the door.

The interior smelled like good leather with a faint hint of expensive cologne. Weirdly nervous, she settled into the passenger seat, her bag placed primly on her lap.

"Can I take that?" He gestured at the bag, and when she nodded, he lifted it off her lap and stretched around to place it on the back seat. She stared, oddly mesmerised by his easy, masculine movements, only tearing her eyes away when he turned back to her, a small smile on his face.

"Now, food. Is there anywhere in particular you'd like to go?"

She shook her head slowly, somehow unable to

put thoughts and memories together enough to decide on a place.

"Why don't you pick?" she said. "I'm not feeling choosy. I could eat anything right now."

He laughed. "I think I know that feeling."

The radio was on some local station, and the host babbled gossip about local musicians in an unidentifiable foreign accent. After a while, a popular track came on. The beat was genius, but the lyrics were just slightly above nonsensical.

"Who writes these songs?" Daniel said, laughing, his words echoing her thoughts. She turned to look at him, watching as his teeth gleamed white in the dark interior of the car. She liked the way he looked, liked the way he threw his head back when he laughed, the way his lips quirked when he noticed she was staring.

She held his gaze for a few seconds before turning back to face the street ahead. "I ask myself that question all the time."

Daniel's head bobbed slightly to the music. "At least they're great to dance to."

"You dance?" The surprise slipped out before she could control it. It was just too hard to imagine… him…letting go on a dance floor.

He quirked a teasing eyebrow in her direction.

"Stick with me and maybe one of these days, you'll see for yourself."

Stick with me.

Ah!

AFTER A SHORT DRIVE, they pulled into the gravel parking area of a restaurant Hope had never heard of. Inside, it was not very large, but the arrangement of the tables was spacious and inviting. The décor was vivid, with local print tablecloths, raffia place settings, and indigenous art on the walls.

A hostess in a pretty ankara dress led them to a dark mahogany table set low to the ground, with a soft leather settee curved around it.

Daniel made sure Hope was seated before settling down and stretching his long legs. Because of the shape of the table and seat, they sat next to each other, almost side by side. Their bodies weren't quite touching, but Hope was intensely aware of how close he was.

A waiter replaced the smiling hostess and offered them menus. Hope opened hers, looking through the pictures of mouth-watering dishes. Daniel was discussing wine, and when he asked if she had any preferences, she shook her head, letting him do the choosing.

"I've been here a few times before, and I can assure you the food is superb," Daniel said, once the waiter had gone.

"I don't doubt it." Hope looked around. The aroma hanging in the air was already doing things to her taste buds. "How did you find this place?"

Daniel thought for a moment. "My assistant, I think, or maybe my siblings. They all recommend places to me from time to time."

"Siblings?" She raised a brow. Somehow, she'd always imagined him alone. It was odd thinking of him with brothers and sisters, playmates... "Older or younger?"

"My sister is older. My brother is much younger."

"Me too," Hope said. "I have a big sister, and my brother is the baby."

Just then the waiter arrived with a bottle of red wine, which he opened with almost comic flair and poured into two glasses, then he took their food orders and disappeared again.

"Did you always know you wanted to be an engineer?" Daniel asked, after they'd exhausted the topic of their families and siblings.

It wasn't the first time she'd been asked the

question. "My dad is one, so there was a time before I knew anything about the profession when I wanted to do it so I could be like him." Hope smiled, remembering that childhood version of herself. "Somewhere before the end of secondary school though, it became real for me. I read a couple of books about famous engineers and after that I couldn't imagine doing anything else."

Daniel was smiling. "Your dad is your hero. That's cool. You didn't think of pursuing your mum's profession?"

"Nursing?" Hope shook her head. "Nope. It never occurred to me. She had crazy shifts when I was younger, and she was always exhausted. Engineering just seemed cooler."

"It is cooler," he said, lips quirking.

"Arguably. Not as many points for saving lives in a direct way though." Hope watched him chuckle. "How about you? Did you always plan to conquer and subjugate the world of information technology in Nigeria?"

His chuckle turned into a laugh, the sound deep and unreserved. "Conquer and subjugate indeed." He shook his head. "That's one way to put it."

Hope smiled and sipped her wine. "Maybe I should have said seize and dominate."

He laughed some more. "You make me sound like an ancient warrior king or something."

Hope tried not to imagine him as exactly that... strong, merciless, seizing control of the world in the brutal past. It was an image that suited him somehow.

"Seriously though," he said, still amused. "I was always into computers and programming. I grew up learning as much as I could, reading books, taking courses right out of secondary school. In Uni, lecturers were struggling to teach things I'd learned years before. I knew I had to leave the country. So, I started giving tutorials, building websites, saving money..." He shrugged. "During my masters..."

"Outside the country?"

He nodded, "The opportunities to learn were so much more, not just in school. Tech companies were doing literally ground-breaking work. I got internships, learned and came back just in time to provide solutions growing businesses were demanding in a recovering economy."

"That's remarkable," Hope said.

He chuckled. "It's my prepared presentation for impressing journalists...and women."

Women...like herself? Her heart quickened at the thought that for any reason, he'd want to impress her.

Just then, the waiter arrived with a tray of steaming dishes. The food smelled divine, and Hope's stomach rumbled with anticipation.

"I don't want to stop," she complained later, when she couldn't take another bite. She looked longingly at the remaining food in the serving bowls. "I want to eat every single bite but I'm too full."

Daniel chuckled. "They try very hard to incapacitate people with food."

"I am incapacitated."

The waiters came to clear the table, then disappeared again, leaving them alone.

"Thanks." Hope sighed drowsily. "That was a wonderful meal."

"I aim to please." He refilled her wineglass, and as she lifted it to her lips, their eyes met and held over the glass. Hope felt her stomach clench. She took a quick sip of the wine, her now familiar awareness of him creating a sweet tension in her limbs.

He leaned back in his seat, his body stretched out and relaxed, unlike hers, which felt wound up and taut. She could feel his eyes on her, and she wondered what he was thinking, and whether he was as attracted to her as she was to him.

"May I ask you something?" His voice was low.

She met his eyes, a quick smile crossing her lips. "Of course."

"The person you were waiting for..." he said slowly. "Boyfriend?"

She thought about Charles, and how, since they'd left the office, she hadn't thought about him, even once, then she shook her head slowly. "No, just a ghost from my past."

"Good," Daniel said.

Hope raised her brows, giving him a sidelong look. "Really?"

He leaned forward, towards her, until his face was close to her own, and even though they weren't making any physical contact, his proximity made her skin tingle.

"I like you," he said softly, his eyes burning with an intensity that made Hope catch her breath. He stopped, then smiled. "Scratch that. I'm very, very attracted to you."

"I..." Hope stammered. Her heart was pounding. Should she tell him she felt the same way? Because she did, but...she closed her eyes, just last night she'd been rekindling things with Charles...

Granted, that had been a mistake, but...was she ready to follow another attraction so soon?

Daniel wasn't waiting for a response. He'd

already leaned back, reclining once again as he drank his wine.

"I'll take you home whenever you're ready," he said quietly.

Hope nodded. There was a little more wine in her glass, and she gulped it down before rising to her feet. Daniel rose too, and suddenly they were standing face to face.

He reached for her face, a finger coming up to wipe something—a drop of wine she'd missed—from the corner of her lips. The finger lingered, and she raised her eyes to his, losing herself immediately in the stormy intensity of his gaze. Her eyes dropped to his lips, and at that moment, she wanted, more than anything for him to kiss her.

His lips curved into a smile and he pulled his hand away. "Ready?" he asked.

Hope nodded. "Yes." And then she followed him out of the restaurant on shaky legs.

CHAPTER NINE

"*I'm very very attracted to you.*"

What did that even mean? Hope wondered later, alone in her bedroom.

What did he want, or expect, and more importantly...what did she want?

She was attracted to him. She'd be lying to herself if she tried to deny that. Her skin tingled just at the thought of him, at the memory of the slightest touch of his fingers...

She closed her eyes and sat at the edge of her bed. After dinner, after that discombobulating revelation that he was attracted to her, he'd driven her home, polite and pleasant as he said goodbye. There had been no hint of a desire for any kind of intimacy, no suggestion of wanting something as simple as a kiss. She'd said goodnight too, questions hovering on her tongue.

And now she couldn't stop thinking about him.

The air from the AC felt cool against her skin. She sighed and lay back on the bed, pulling the duvet over her body. She had work tomorrow, so she needed sleep, but just before she finally let go of thoughts of Daniel and drifted off, she realised with satisfaction, how little thought she'd given to Charles throughout the night.

SHE WAS STILL THINKING of that the next morning when she got to work. She wished she could call Charles and throw the fact in his face. *You mean nothing to me. It only took one evening to forget that you ever came back into my life.*

She wondered if he would even care. It hurt to think of how easily she'd been dragged back into that space of wanting him and doubting herself.

But she was done with all that now.

She kept an eye out for Daniel in the lobby, but to her disappointment, she didn't run into him on her way to her office. During the day, her mind kept wandering back to him, back to their evening together, and she went over every single word he'd said.

I'm very very attracted to you.

They had made no arrangements to see each other again, and it nagged at her, because he intrigued her.

At lunchtime, she ordered a Chinese takeaway and ate at her desk. Then, with about thirty minutes to spare, she did a little online shopping and checked her social media accounts.

"You have a delivery."

Hope looked up from her computer to see Ladi, her least favourite of the two front desk receptionists. Ladi was older, married, and believed she was superior to any unmarried girl, even the engineers. She bullied her fellow receptionist, Joy, and barely hid her disdain for Hope and Agnes.

"Thanks." Hope smiled politely. She opened the package and pulled out a box of Belgian chocolates wrapped with ribbons tied in a bow. There was a note under the bow.

Hope stared at the note, hesitant. It was probably Charles's half-assed attempt at an apology, and she wasn't sure she had time for that.

She opened the note.

It wasn't from Charles.

The words were in a firm, slanted handwriting she had never seen before.

"Had a great time last night. Been out of the office all day but I was thinking of you. Daniel."

Hope stared at the words and flushed with pleasure. Ladi was still standing there, trying to read the words on the note.

"Thank you," Hope said pointedly.

The other woman pursed her lips. "Thank God for your life o. At least you have admirer."

Hope swallowed an annoyed retort, unwilling to let the other woman ruin her pleasure. Ladi walked away and Hope made a face at her retreating back.

"Yay! Chocolates!" Agnes exclaimed, and hastily, Hope put the note inside her desk drawer. She wasn't ready to talk about Daniel with anyone, not yet, and not even with Agnes.

"Who're they from?" Agnes asked, coming over to lean on Hope's desk.

"A guy."

Agnes gave her a look. "Okay o! If you don't want to tell me, at least give me small chocolate make I chop."

Hope laughed and opened the box of chocolates, taking a few of them for herself, before handing the rest over to Agnes to share with the others. She would have liked to send Daniel a text to say thank you, but she realised that she didn't have his number, and he didn't have hers.

That was awkward.

By the close of day, she still hadn't seen him, and she wondered if he had been out of the office all day. It was just as well. She could imagine the furore it would cause among her colleagues if he showed up at the office looking for her, or if he called the front desk and asked to speak to her. A huge mountain that would be made out of that molehill.

She got ready to go home, freshening her makeup while telling herself that it wasn't because she hoped she would run into him in the downstairs lobby.

As soon as she stepped out of the lift on the ground floor, her eyes scanned the lobby, expectation making her chest tight.

He wasn't there.

She was being silly. He was a busy man. It wasn't like he was the kind of person who had the time to hang around in the lobby hoping that she would walk by. When he wanted to talk to her or see her, he would probably make it happen.

She started towards the entrance, slowing her steps as she passed the seating area, still hoping he'd be there. He wasn't. Sighing, she continued outside.

"Excuse me."

She whirled around at the sound of Daniel's voice, then cursed herself for being too eager, too excited. He was standing behind her, wearing a light grey shirt with the sleeves rolled up to his elbows, just like the night before, with pants that showed off his trim figure and long legs. A mischievous smile danced on his lips even as he tried to keep a straight face.

"Excuse me," he said again, still trying to keep the smile off his face. "My name is Daniel Amadi, and I work in the building. I've noticed you around, and I'd like to get to know you better. Can I have your number, so we can...maybe talk?" He managed a hopeful expression for effect.

Hope burst into laughter. "I'll give you my number if you admit that those lines are terrible and would never work on any girl who didn't already know you."

"You think?" He was laughing. "That was the standard pickup speech when I was in secondary school."

"I'm concluding it hardly ever worked."

He quirked an eyebrow. The mischievous smile was back. "I'm not telling."

Hope gave him a pointed look, and his grin widened. "I had lines," he said. "Good ones." He studied her face. "So seriously, I'd like to have your number."

Hope nodded. "Of course. I was thinking about that earlier. How I couldn't call you if I wanted."

He wiggled his eyebrows. "You wanted to call me?"

Hope blushed. "Just to thank you for the chocolates."

"Hmmm." He smiled, his teasing expression making Hope roll her eyes.

"I'm working late tonight," he said, after they exchanged numbers. There was a note of apology in his voice. "But I'll call you later. Do you mind?"

Of course not! "No, I don't," Hope said. "Thanks for last night...and the chocolates."

He winked. "I told you," he said, backing away. "I aim to please."

She watched him go, sure that she had a foolish grin on her face. She turned back towards the entrance, unable to stop smiling as she walked outside. In the parking lot, her phone beeped, and when she unlocked the screen. There was a new message.

"I didn't tell you how great you look. You look beautiful. Daniel."

Now there was absolutely no way she would be able to wipe the smile off her face.

WHEN SHE GOT HOME, she noticed her brother's car parked beside her mother's. Excited to see him, she hurried into the house. Her parents were in the living room, with Gerald seated on the arm of their mother's chair, showing her pictures on his tablet, while she smiled indulgently, the way she always did when her only son was around.

"Who is this troublemaker?" Hope said, walking into the living room.

Gerald looked up and his face split in a grin. He was taller than Hope, slightly darker, but their features were very alike. He was handsome, and he knew it.

"Popo!" he exclaimed, using the name he'd called her when he was a baby learning to talk. He wrapped her in a hug, then pulled away to peer at her face. "You're looking very pleased with yourself," he noted suspiciously.

"It's God," Hope replied with a shrug, while her mind went back to Daniel's text. "What are you doing home?"

"I was missing you guys. Decided to bless you people with one night of my busy life."

"Seriously," Hope rolled her eyes. "You're so full

of yourself. Nobody considers your presence a blessing."

"I do, please," Their mother said. "I'm ecstatic to see him."

"Thanks mum." Gerald smiled smugly. "I've missed pissing you off," he said to Hope.

"I've missed your empty head," she teased.

Later, after she'd changed out of her work clothes, she returned downstairs for dinner. It had been a while since dinner at home included anyone but she and her parents, so having Gerald to share stories from his work in the legal department of one of the biggest auditing firms in the country was a rare treat.

"How's that your friend from Law school?" their mother asked. "That pretty girl that finished with a first class?"

"Lara?"

"I think so."

"Oh. She's fine," Gerald said. "She's getting married next month."

Their mother paused. "What of David?" She asked, naming another friend.

"I haven't heard from him in a while, but he's living in Canada with his wife. Had a kid a while back."

"His parents are so lucky."

Hope gave Gerald a look, and they both rolled their eyes. Even their father couldn't resist a chuckle.

Their mother shook her head. "I don't know which one of you two is worse. Settling down is not a curse. It's a good thing. If not for Grace that has consented to give me grandchildren, I don't know what I would do with the two of you."

Their father looked from Hope and Gerald to his wife. "Patience, let them eat."

She huffed but didn't push it.

"You're lucky you still live at home," Gerald said later, when they were upstairs in her room. "Home-cooked meals and free house help."

"Sometimes, I don't think it's worth the freedom of having my own place, especially when Mum starts with all her marriage wahala."

Gerald laughed. "You know if you really wanted to move out, they won't stop you. They'd just be sad and lonely."

Hope eyed him with pursed lips. "So, I'm the loneliness alleviation child."

He ignored her. "I saw that your former boyfriend about a week ago. Charles something. He came for a meeting in my office."

Hope was quiet. "Did you talk to him?"

He frowned. "No. I don't think he recognised me. He was flirting with one of my colleagues after the meeting. I almost decked him. I still remember how he made you cry for like six months straight when he messed up."

Flirting with one of Gerald's colleagues. She wasn't surprised. A week ago. Even while he'd been telling her how much he'd missed her, he still had time to flirt with someone else.

"Forget about him. He's really not worth thinking about," she whispered, more to herself than to Gerald.

They talked some more, before Gerald, who was spending the night, went to sleep in his old room. His visit had been spur of the moment, so he still had to go to his place to change before going to work, meaning, he had to leave very early.

Hope took a quick shower before changing into her nightclothes. As soon as she climbed into bed, her phone started to ring.

"Did I wake you?" Daniel's voice was deep and smooth.

"No." It was odd, how happy she was to hear from him. Little petals of pleasure unfurled in her belly. "I just got into bed."

"Hmm." His deep voice vibrated through the phone and she felt it like a tingle under her skin, in her fingers and her toes. "I got home a few minutes ago, and I wanted to say goodnight before it was too late."

"Now is perfect. My brother's home, so I stayed up talking with him."

"Lucky you. I'm alone here. I wish I saw my family more, but they don't have time for an old workaholic like me."

"You're not old," Hope protested.

"Ah..." he laughed softly, the warm sound filling her ears. "but I'm a workaholic, right?"

"I didn't say that."

"You didn't not say it." He paused. "Did you get my text?"

"Yes," Hope smiled. "Thanks. You didn't look too bad yourself."

He laughed. "Thank you. I don't get complimented on my good looks often enough."

She knew he was joking, but she didn't laugh. "Maybe I should remedy that," she said.

She heard him breathe. "Hope," he whispered. She liked the way he said her name...as if he liked the way it sounded on his lips. "Hope," he said again. "Will you have lunch with me tomorrow?"

She smiled. "Depends. Will you take me somewhere as nice as the last place?"

"Somewhere even better," he promised. "And

while we're there, you can tell me how hot and irresistible you think I look."

"I'll make sure to do that," Hope laughed. "See you tomorrow then."

There was a short pause on his end. "I can't wait," he said finally.

To be honest, neither could she.

CHAPTER TEN

In front of the mirror the next morning, Hope spent more time than usual on her appearance. She wanted to look great, but not like she was trying too hard. For clothes, she chose a black silk blouse and a grey pencil skirt, pairing them with simple jewellery and black velvet pumps. With light make-up, it was a simple but classy look.

By the time she got downstairs, her brother was long gone. She drove to the office, not really minding the crawling traffic. Throughout the morning, there was an intense excitement she couldn't shake as she waited for her lunchtime date with Daniel.

Just before noon, his name lit up the screen of her phone.

"Hello."

"Hey."

"So...when can you meet me downstairs?"

Hope calculated. "About five minutes past noon?"

"Okay. I'll be waiting."

Her excitement intensified. She freshened her makeup. A few minutes later, she checked the clock on the computer screen. Noon at last. She started to get up and saw Agnes studying her.

"You're looking really...chic today," Agnes said. "Are you going out to lunch? Maybe we can grab something together."

"No, sorry. I'm meeting someone."

"Hmmm," Agnes smirked. "Chocolate someone?"

Hope rolled her eyes but didn't deny.

"You will still give me this gist one day," Agnes said playfully. "Enjoy."

A few minutes later, Hope took the lift to the ground floor. Just as she stepped outside the building, a black-tinted SUV pulled up to the entrance. One of the rear windows wound down, and she saw Daniel in the back seat. He beckoned to her, then leant over to open the door.

She joined him in the back, loving the plush, luxurious, black leather interior. In the front, the driver kept his eyes ahead, not saying anything beyond a quiet *good afternoon.*"

"Hey," Daniel said, his dark eyes lit with pleasure as they scanned her face. "How do you look this good every day?"

"It just happens naturally," Hope replied with a playful shrug. She could hardly take her eyes off his gorgeousness in a perfectly tailored charcoal suit. "You look great too."

He frowned. "I was hoping for far more than that. I was promised I'd be told that I'm the sexiest man alive."

Hope laughed. "I promised no such thing."

"Oookay." He made a gesture of surrender then angled his body towards her and leaned forward. "How was work?"

She exhaled slowly, momentarily mesmerised by his nearness. "So, so."

"Hmm." His eyes lingered on hers, then he smiled to himself and leant back in his seat.

"What are you thinking?" Hope asked.

His smile widened. "I'll probably tell you, but not today."

The restaurant he chose was another small one, tucked into a corner of one the luxury event centres on the island. Lunch was a juicy shawarma coupled with a fruit and veggie smoothie.

Hope wrinkled her nose at the tall glass filled with the smooth green drink. "I've never warmed to green smoothies," she said, dubious. "I can't get past that mental block that says veggies should be eaten cooked, in soups."

Daniel laughed. "Try this one. Trust me. You'll love the energy kick you'll get from it."

"Okay." She made a face and took a sip, prepared to beckon to the waiter and request a real drink instead. At the first sip though, her eyes widened. "It's good."

"Right?" Daniel's smile was triumphant. "Seems I have an idea what you like."

Hope swallowed and met his gaze, wondering if she had imagined the sexual undertone.

"Have some more," he said, his voice light. "Tell me what you like about it."

She did as he asked. "I love the sweet fruity base..." she looked at Daniel, who was smiling, seeming as interested in her impression of the drink as if she were talking about something far more significant. "...and how it takes all the blandness away from the greens." Hope laughed. "Who would have ever thought I'd taste a blended leaf and think of the flavour as rich?"

"Me, apparently."

Hope watched him take a bite out of his Sharwama and lean back as he enjoyed the food. His relaxed, easy confidence, his attention to her, his interest in getting to know her...It was all so new, and so different from Charles.

With Charles, she knew how much she'd once wanted him and how easy it would be to settle back into the familiarity of being with him...and that knowledge had driven her desire.

With Daniel, she felt the possibility of real intimacy, not just sex. He wouldn't be satisfied until he knew her inside and out.

The thought scared her. Inside and out. What would he find if he delved too deep?

Someone who wasn't sure she was over Charles? Someone who was afraid of the possibility of new feelings for a man who seemed almost too good to be true, but who, Hope was starting to realise, could well be the most attractive man she'd ever known.

"Your food will get cold." Daniel's voice tore her from her thoughts. He was watching her, almost as if he knew what she'd been thinking.

Hope chuckled. "I'm sorry. I got lost in my thoughts for a minute."

"I have to do a better job of keeping you in the moment then," he said.

And he did. She'd never laughed that much over food. Daniel teased her about her love for romantic movies when she admitted that Love Actually was her favourite movie of all time. He admitted a fixation on Nollywood Movies featuring a particular set of the old-school actors and actresses. "Give me Genevieve, or Rita, or Ramsey, and I'll watch, no matter what the story is."

"Most guys would never admit that," Hope teased.

"Who cares? What people think has never mattered much to me." He shrugged. "I also watch other kinds of movies, superhero movies, action blockbusters, quirky comedies, Hollywood oldies... I'm a cinema nerd."

She stared into his face, wondering at the relaxed, approachable expression, so at odds with the impression she'd had of him for a long time. "It's kind of weird talking to you like this," she admitted. "A few weeks ago, I'd have sworn that you'd probably only talk about work and never crack a smile."

He sipped his drink with a thoughtful expression. "Hope, you know what they say about judging a book by its cover?"

She nodded.

He gave her a long level look. "Never do that."

I LIKE HIM.

I really like him.

Back at the office, Hope couldn't stop thinking about Daniel. Getting to know him would be a pleasure. It would be so easy to fall in love with a guy like him.

And why not? He'd already admitted that he was interested in her.

The more she thought about it, the more it seemed like an attractive prospect, except...

Except for the fact that just a few days ago, she'd been considering a relationship with another man, a man she'd loved for years, a man she thought she'd gotten over, but who had pushed through most of her defences with very little effort.

She was over Charles now, at least she thought she was, but it wouldn't be fair to Daniel to jump right into a relationship with him.

At least, not until she was absolutely certain that she would never lapse into thinking Charles could mean something to her, ever again.

She knew Daniel was not the kind of man who would accept anything less.

I'm very very attracted to you.

Hope sighed. Just remembering the words and the way he'd said them made her tremble a little.

She was *very very* attracted to him too.

The day passed quickly. There was an unscheduled visit to a nearby building site to inspect some piping ducts the project manager claimed the contractor had installed without following the specifications. A long meeting followed the inspection, with tiring arguments filled with raised voices and denials from the contractor, Hope returned to the office exhausted. By then it was almost closing time.

"I can't wait for weekend," Agnes said, stretching as she got up. "Sometimes I don't know if I want the days to speed up, so the weekends and salaries can come faster, or if I want them to slow down, so I stay young and beautiful for longer."

Hope thought about it. "Who knew there was a philosopher under all your man craziness?"

Agnes giggled. "I like the idea of me as a deep thinker."

"I don't know who told you you're even young and beautiful now," Jide, one of their colleagues said to Agnes. He and Agnes had a friendship that mainly consisted of teasing barbs and sparring, but Hope suspected that his feelings towards Agnes were a little more than professional courtesy.

Agnes glanced at him and pursed her lips. "I don't know who was talking to you o, Jide."

He held up his hands. "Somebody cannot joke with you again." Agnes made a face at him, and Hope laughed.

"How far with that your full package guy?" she asked, lowering her voice.

Agnes made a sour face. "Bayo? He didn't call me again. Just like that, almost a week of complete attention, then silence."

Hope raised her brows. "For real?"

Agnes nodded. "I finally called him, and he gave me some lame excuses about work and being busy. I think he has a wife or a fiancée or something. What can I say? Men are scum." She paused for a moment, then threw off her sad expression and brightened. "I've moved on sha. I've started seeing someone else. I'll tell you about him, but I don't think it's serious. Maybe casual is what I need, really. I'm tired of trying for love. So...on to the next one, abi?"

Or give it a break for a while? Take some time off from men before jumping into the next guy's arms?

She held off on advising Agnes, because, to be truthful, she probably needed the advice more. Here she was, the stain of Charles's kisses still almost fresh on her lips, and she was already thinking of starting something new with Daniel.

"As long as you're happy," she offered.

Agnes shrugged. "I'm okay. Sometimes, that's all you get."

Moments later, Hope's phone beeped. Agnes had gone toward the restrooms, and Hope spared her a thoughtful glance before looking at the message. It was from Daniel.

"*Just got back. Have you left yet?*"

"*No. How was your meeting?*"

"*Govt officials. *angry face**"

"*I can imagine.*"

"*When are you leaving?*"

"*In about an hour and a half. I'm going to wait for traffic to taper off.*"

"*Let me know when you're ready to leave.*"

"*Okay.*"

Hope wondered why he wanted to know, and excitement fluttered in her belly. She didn't think he would ask her to join him for dinner, or else he'd have said so.

Well, she'd find out when she saw him.

She decided to focus on work instead of marinating herself endlessly in her thoughts about him. So, once the office emptied out, she retrieved her laptop from her bag and focused on the mechanical drawings she was producing for a personal client for a small residential development.

After almost two hours, she realised it was getting dark outside. She packed her things, quickly dabbing powder on her nose and reapplying her lip gloss before sending Daniel a message to let him know that she was ready to leave.

He met her in the lobby on her floor, stepping out of the lift just as she exited her office. She stopped walking when she saw him, wondering again at how he filled the whole place with his presence. He'd discarded his jacket as he usually did in the evenings and was once again wearing only a tailored shirt and pants. This time though, the sleeves weren't rolled up.

He came towards her, fast but graceful, and relieved her of the laptop pouch.

"This is heavy," he exclaimed. "What kind of machine are you working with?'

She laughed. "Just a regular laptop. And I know it's not that heavy."

He pressed the button for the lift, chuckling. "How about that one," he asked, nodding towards her handbag. "Do you need help with that?"

She gave him a side-eye. "You'd carry my handbag?"

"Why not?" He grinned. "If you care about stuff like that, you'd probably be more embarrassed than me, anyway. I told you, I'm not very good at caring what people think."

Hope had no doubt that he didn't need others to validate his opinions, but she knew that if people in the lobby saw him carrying her bags, the whole building would talk about it for days. "I can manage," she said, chuckling. "Thanks for offering."

The lift arrived, and soon they were on their way to the ground floor. Alone with him inside the small space, Hope remembered that first day, when he'd picked up the purse she'd dropped on the floor. She remembered the connection she'd felt, the unexplainable frisson of excitement. There'd been something there, between them, even then.

He was watching her now, and his eyes lowered to her lips, then he looked back up into her eyes.

I'm very very attracted to you.

The words resounded in her head, and she swallowed, sure that he knew what she was thinking, or at least that she was thinking of how attracted she was to him.

His eyes held hers, and she could feel her stomach tensing and flipping. He leaned in her direction, almost as if he was going to take a step and close the space between them, then he seemed to think better of it, and shoved his free hand into his pocket.

"Are you seeing anyone?" he asked.

She breathed. *No,* she wanted to say. There's no one. No one important. No one unimportant either. No one at all. Charles doesn't matter.

Why had her mind gone to Charles?

Maybe because he still mattered?

He hadn't called, and even if he did, she knew he wasn't worth her time.

But did that mean she was ready for something else? Ready for Daniel?

"Are you?" She countered with a tiny smile, her chin lifting.

Daniel chuckled, looking away from her face for the first time since they entered the lift. There was a beep as they reached the ground floor, and the doors slid open. He let her lead the way, following her out, his free hand hovering at the small of her back, there—enough for her to feel a warm burn as if he was actually touching her, enough for her to go almost crazy with the desire for him to rest that hand on her bare skin. The hand dropped as soon as they entered the main area of the lobby. He looked at her, his black eyes burning and intense.

"I'm not seeing anyone," he murmured.

She wondered if she could believe him. He was incredibly good-looking, painfully rich, extremely eligible. Men like him were hardly ever single. There was always some girl.

"I'm not seeing anyone either." It was the truth, but it felt incomplete, somehow. She could feel her connection with Charles, renewed in the past few weeks, like a frayed string she hadn't yet fully cut.

They went outside together, walking to where she had parked her car in the small lot. It was a cool evening, and Hope felt the temptation to lean into him as they walked.

Slow down, she cautioned herself desperately. *Hope, slow down.*

Daniel waited while she fished out her keys and unlocked the car doors, then he went around the back of the car and placed the laptop pouch on the floor of the front passenger's side.

"Just so none of the robbers in traffic sees it and shatters your windows for it."

"You're right," she said, shuddering as she recalled stories of vicious armed robbers lurking in the Lagos traffic. She walked over to where Daniel was standing and placed her handbag on top of the laptop pouch. When she straightened, they were standing face to face, with too little space between their bodies. Her heart thudded, but she met his gaze squarely.

His eyes held hers. "I'm becoming very addicted to being around you."

She bit her lower lip. "Is that a bad thing?"

"Depends."

"On what?"

In response, he lifted a hand, gently cupping it around the back of her neck. Hope bit back a sigh, pleasure at his touch mingling with the excitement low in her belly. Her lips parted as he lowered his head. His lips touched hers, and she felt a jolt, a rush of pleasure as her whole body melted into the kiss.

There was no pressure, just his hand at her nape and his lips on hers, sweet, tender, undemanding, and yet so pleasurable she wanted to press her whole body against his, to burrow into him, to deepen the kiss until there was nothing left between them.

But he was holding back, limiting himself to this tender exploration. A small moan escaped her, and she felt him stiffen, his fingers flexed, the tips sliding into the back of her hair. The kiss deepened, only for a moment, then he was pulling away, leaving her unsteady on her feet.

She pressed her lips together, rocked by an unrelenting wave of pleasure. Daniel had taken a step back, and he looked as if he was waiting for her to say something. But what could she say? Her legs were still trembling... and it had been just one kiss. She knew she was attracted to him, but she hadn't expected that surge of physical pleasure—that almost-uncontrollable desire to melt into him...to surrender everything.

She could really fall for this man. He listened. He spoke to her as if she was a person, not just an attractive woman. He was unarguably brilliant, interesting and attractive. It would be too easy to fall...

But...so soon after Charles?

The thought of Charles soured her mind. What if, like Charles, Daniel was just playing around? She would get hurt, and she'd still have to face working with him in the same building.

She took a step back, recoiling, not from him, but from her feelings, from the doubts that had taken root inside her mind.

"It's getting late," she said, her voice weak. "I really should be going."

He regarded her in silence for what seemed like a long time. "You're right." He stepped back from the car and closed the passenger door, watching her as she walked over to the driver's side. She opened the door and paused, looking over the roof of the car at him. "I..." she started, then frowned, not sure what to say. "Goodnight, Daniel."

"Goodnight."

She slid into the car and started the engine. As she drove away, she glimpsed him in the rear-view mirror. He was watching her go, his hands shoved into his pockets, an indecipherable expression on his face.

CHAPTER ELEVEN

"Auntie Hope, do you want a massage?" It was Diana, her six-year-old niece, hovering at the door to her mother's bedroom, where Hope and her sister Grace were talking, or trying to.

"Maybe later," Hope replied, smiling fondly at the little girl. According to Grace, Diana recently saw a massage programme on TV and decided she wanted to give everyone back massages which were usually just hard punches with her small fists.

"Later when?"

"Later, Di," Grace said with her stern mummy voice. "Leave Mummy and Auntie Hope alone to talk."

"But I want to talk too," Diana replied, folding small arms across her chest.

"Go downstairs and watch TV with daddy."

"He's watching football...!" Diana complained, but she obeyed, closing the door and leaving Hope alone with her sister.

"These children can kill somebody." Grace sighed. She was shorter than Hope, a little plumper, with a no-nonsense demeanour toward her younger siblings that had kept Hope and Gerald in line when they were younger. "I haven't had a real weekend since I had the first one, I swear." She looked at Hope. "So, as we were saying..."

Hope had been telling her about the events of the past few weeks, Charles, the party, the dinner at his apartment, then Daniel and everything that had happened between them.

Grace sighed. "And Charles hasn't called you till now?"

Hope shook her head.

"At least you're not making excuses for him, trying to reach him *in case he had an accident* or those other kinds of excuses you used to make for him back then." Grace patted Hope's hand. "I never liked him. I think he's the worst kind of man and I'm a little disappointed that you let him back into your life at all."

Hope stuck out her lower lip. "Are you going to judge me?"

"I'm trying not to." Grace yawned. "I like this Daniel though. He seems like a nice guy."

"I think he is, but I don't want to rush into anything. Given what *almost* happened with Charles, I don't trust myself to make the right decisions right now. Maybe I'm just lonely, or maybe it's Mum's marriage talk getting to my head, you know?"

Grace chuckled. "I understand. He's there, he's attracted to you...It's easy to jump into something you're not ready for."

Hope remembered the kiss in the car park and pulled in a breath. "Exactly."

"Have you asked yourself what you'll do if Charles comes back now, apologising, with a good explanation? If you find out he's single now, and you two can be together...would you want to be with him?"

Hope imagined the possibility of everything she used to want so desperately, all the hopes Charles had rekindled in the short period he'd come back into her life, it was tempting...

...but then she remembered all the lies, the betrayals, the pain...everything she'd foolishly forgotten just because he'd returned with his charm and his lies.

"No," she answered, shaking her head. She met

Grace's assessing gaze. "No," she said again, her voice firmer this time. "I believe I'm done with him, finally."

Grace looked proud. "I'm glad."

"Me too." Hope thought for a moment. "I don't think I'll ever forgive him for what he did to me, but I know for sure I never want to be with him again."

Grace studied her face for a moment, then shrugged. "I think you should give yourself a little more time to get to know Daniel...make sure he likes you for you...that he's not a player...though from your description, he doesn't sound like one."

"He doesn't give me the player vibe at all."

"What vibe does he give you?"

Hope thought for a moment. "Serious but playful...Intense."

"Hmm," Grace thought. "Not too serious though, hopefully. Some guys are players while some are so serious about settling down that they don't care about getting to know you, they only care about the idea of you and all the 'qualities' they've convinced themselves that you have."

Hope gave her sister a worried frown. "You think that's what this is? He wants to settle down, and he *picked me*?"

Grace chuckled. "Calm down. I think he really likes you and wants to get to know you." She gave

Hope a reassuring smile. "Anyway, I hope it works out, and then who knows...maybe we'll finally come and eat rice at your wedding."

"Ha! Please don't let mummy hear o, before she starts planning the wedding in her head."

The door opened again and Diana poked her head inside and gazed at her mother with imploring eyes. Grace laughed and went to the door to swoop the little girl up into her arms, kissing her all over her cheeks. "Are you missing mummy?"

Diana squirmed and laughed happily. "Let's go downstairs," Grace said, beckoning to Hope. "If my baby's team loses, he will need some consoling."

On their way downstairs, Grace still carrying Diana, Hope's phone rang. The sight of Daniel's name on the screen made her stomach flip.

She touched the screen, noticing the tiny tremble in her fingers as she pulled in a small breath. "Hello."

"Hi." As usual, the depth and timbre of his voice went straight from her ears to other parts of her body. For the thousandth time, her mind flooded with memories of the kiss at the car park. She hadn't seen him or spoken to him since then. The intensity of her reaction to him was making her cautious, and she wondered if he felt the same way.

"How're you doing?" he asked.

"I'm fine." She hovered on the stairs. "I'm at my sister's."

"Grace," he said. "The doctor."

He remembered. Hope felt a fluttering of pleasure at that small detail. "Yes. What about you? What are you doing?"

"Watching the match with some friends."

"You're not watching it if you're talking to me," she teased.

He laughed. "I'm multitasking—and anyway, I don't have to watch the full ninety minutes. If I miss anything important, there's always a replay."

Hope faked a gasp. "I'm shocked. You're no true football fan."

"I admit I'm not as obsessed as some," Daniel replied, chuckling. "So...are you spending the whole day at your sister's or should I come over and steal you right now?"

"Umm." Hope paused. The offer was tempting but...she knew she had to exercise caution with him, and that meant taking it slow. If she spent too much time with him, things would move fast, and it was likely they'd move out of her control.

"Ummmm..." he prompted gently.

"I'm a bit tired," she said, wondering if she was making a mistake. "I think I'm just going to go home and rest."

"Oh." She heard the hint of disappointment in his voice. "Okay. I'm crushed, but I'll console myself with a win from my team." There was a pause. "Take care of yourself."

"I'll try to."

"I'm serious."

"Okay." She smiled. "I *will* take care of myself."

"I'll see you," he said. "Enjoy your weekend."

"You too," Hope replied, feeling as if she'd messed up somehow, because the truth was, she'd have loved to see him.

After an early night on Saturday, she was up early on Sunday. She went to church with her parents and spent the rest of the day trying to read a novel, but was too distracted by her thoughts, which kept straying to Daniel.

What did he think about her refusal to see him the day before? Had she hurt his pride? She was certain that girls rarely turned him down for dates or hangouts or whatever. Would he think she was playing hard to get? She hoped not—that wasn't her style.

By evening she'd dozed, made little progress reading her novel and finally started picking out clothes to wear for the week. Her phone rang for a few seconds before she heard it, and by the time she picked it up the call had ended. It was Daniel.

Great! She sighed. Now he would think she didn't want to talk to him.

To her relief, the ringing started again, and she quickly answered the call.

"Hey," she said.

"Hey," his voice vibrated through the phone, deep and delicious. "How are you?"

"I'm good." She had a sudden longing to see him, to watch him smile his crooked smile, to hear him laugh. She closed her eyes and took a deep breath. "I'm trying to get ready for tomorrow."

"When the grind begins again..." he said wryly.

"You get it," Hope replied with a sigh. "So...did your team win yesterday?"

"Of course," he said, sounding as proud as if he had anything to do with the win. "We always win."

Hope laughed. "That's impossible."

"Impossible is nothing," he replied. There was a pause. "How're you feeling today?"

He sounded concerned, and Hope felt her heart tighten with something like guilt. "I'm okay."

"Hmm." He seemed to be considering something. "I need you to do me a favour," he said. "Scratch that—two favours. Number two, I have a question, and I need you to answer it truthfully. Can you do that?"

Her stomach tensed. "Depends on the question."

"Fair enough. It's not a big deal."

"Ookay." She paused. "What's number one."

"Can you come outside your gate?"

"You're here?" Hope ran to her bedroom window, trying to see the street beyond the fence.

"Yes, I am."

Her heart started to thud, and she forgot about taking it slow. "I'll be right there."

He had parked right outside the gate, seated inside a gleaming blue Audi-something—she didn't know car models well enough to say what exactly it was. As she walked over, he got out of the car, long-legged, fit and achingly good-looking in a cream Henley, jeans and aviators.

They hugged lightly. She could have stayed in his arms forever, but he only gave her a moment to fill her lungs with his cologne before stepping back and opening the passenger door for her.

She slid into the car, and a few seconds later, he joined her. He took off his glasses and turned to face her, leaving her a little light-headed just from looking at his face.

His lips curved, and without saying anything to her, he started singing along to the song playing on the radio—one of BankyW's love songs—and it felt like he was singing the words to her. It was something about what she was doing to his heart, or what some girl was doing to the musician's heart—Hope couldn't be sure, the warmth in his eyes made her too confused to think.

"You don't look as happy to see me as I hoped," he teased.

Her heart fluttered. Happy wasn't the word she'd have used to describe how she was feeling—confused, excited, tense, hot and cold and warm at the same time...? "I'm just surprised," she said evenly. "I wasn't expecting you."

"Yeah," he exhaled. "I wasn't expecting me to be here either." He drummed his fingers on the armrest. "I just...I found myself really wanting to see you."

Hope swallowed. "I..." What could she say to that? She was flattered, pleased and a lot more she couldn't articulate. "Why?" she asked.

His eyes bored into hers, piercing, intense, intimate... He started to lean forward, then stopped himself. "I had a question I needed to ask."

"Okay." Hope looked from his face to her hands on her lap. The music had changed to another love song, the sound blending with the low purr of the engine and the AC. Outside, the sun was setting, and a few people were walking along the street, but there was a sense of intimacy within the car that made it seem almost like they were alone in the world. "I said I'll answer it if I can."

"You can." He gave her a measuring look. "Why didn't you want to see me yesterday?"

Of course, Hope thought. He didn't buy the lie she'd told about being tired. His eyes were on her face now, and she knew repeating the lie would only insult his intelligence.

She chewed her bottom lip. "It's complicated."

He was silent. She met his gaze, and it seemed as if he was challenging her to say more, but she didn't. The source of her confusion was murky, even to her, and she couldn't yet put it into words.

He was still waiting. The silence stretched. Hope searched her head for something to say, something to lighten the mood, but she came up with nothing.

"Hope."

She pulled in a small breath at the sound of her name on his lips. "You know what's not complicated?" he asked softly.

Hope shook her head.

"I like you," he said. "I'm a busy man, Hope. There are a lot of things I could be doing right now, a lot of places I could be, but here, with you, is where I want to be, because I enjoy being around you, and more than anything, I want you to feel the same about me."

Hope sighed. "Daniel..."

"I'm not done." He studied her face. "I don't think you're the type who likes to play unnecessary games. I think you like me too. If you didn't, you wouldn't be here, and neither would I." He paused. "So, whatever your reasons for pulling back, I'm guessing they're valid."

"They are."

He took her hand in his and traced his fingers over hers. "Do you want me to leave you alone?"

At the thought, she felt pain stab through her insides. She swallowed and looked at her hand nestled in his. "Would you?"

He grinned. "No. I'm very patient." There was a pause. "But I won't wait forever either."

"I don't expect you to."

"Fair enough." He let go of her fingers, and she pulled them back onto her lap, feeling the absence of his touch. "What are your plans for the rest of the day?"

"Sleep, then I'll get ready for work tomorrow."

He nodded. "I guess I'll see you tomorrow then."

Hope bit her lip. He was leaving then, but what had she expected? She'd practically told him she didn't want him around, at least not how he wanted to be.

She opened the door and stepped out of the car, surprised when Daniel did the same. He came around to where she was standing. Curious, she waited for him to say something.

He pulled her into a small hug and placed a tiny kiss on her cheek. "Take care," he whispered gently.

She nodded and walked into the compound, leaving him outside the gates. *Take care.* Why did it sound so much like goodbye?

CHAPTER TWELVE

HOPE DIDN'T SEE Daniel throughout the next week. She didn't hear from him at all, and even though she thought about calling him a few times, she always hesitated, because, after all, she'd told him she wasn't ready to have him in her life.

What if he'd decided he didn't want to wait for her after all?

The thought filled her with a vague sense of loss. He probably had loads of girls at his beck and call. Why would he hold on for the one who was dragging her feet for no apparent reason?

By Friday afternoon, she still hadn't heard from him. She was beginning to despair, and all her thoughts now seemed focused on him.

Had she sabotaged something good with him just

because she couldn't let go of the memory of Charles?

The possibility was upsetting.

As soon as people started leaving for lunch, she reached for her phone, intending to call him, but before she could, it started to buzz.

It wasn't Daniel. It was Ebisan Cassidy. Hope swallowed the deep feeling of disappointment. Ebisan was a close friend from university days, but in the years since school they'd seen less of each other, mainly because of their jobs and the demands of Lagos life.

"Hello, babe." Hope said, feeling just a tiny bit guilty for wishing she was speaking to Daniel instead.

"Hope! What's up? How's work?"

"Sensational. How are you?"

"I'm fine," Ebisan replied. "Long time no see."

"It's work. You know how it is."

"I know." Ebisan sighed. "Lagos life is stressful. Anyway, I need to ask you...what are you doing this weekend?"

Hope thought about Daniel and felt hurt squeeze her chest area. "I don't know. Nothing. Why?"

"Well...Tunde's birthday is next week..."

"Yay!"

Ebisan laughed. "But he'll be travelling the day before, so I decided to arrange a small soiree for him this Saturday evening. It's a surprise."

Tunde and Ebisan had been married for four years and had a toddler and a little baby. Hope imagined that for them the party would be a much-needed break from baby talk and diapers.

"A party sounds exciting," Hope said.

"Hmm mmm, and you're invited. Oceanside restaurant. Saturday evening at five. We're getting a large table. Some people from school days will be there too. I don't know if you remember Tunde's cousin Dennis? He was at our wedding. I introduced you guys."

So, there would be an attempt to hook her up with someone at the party. "I think I have a faint memory, but I'm not sure."

Ebisan laughed. "Well, he'll be there, maybe you guys will catch up, or something."

Or something. After the call, it occurred to Hope that Ebisan hadn't asked if Hope was seeing someone or not. It was funny, as long as you weren't married, people didn't hesitate to set you up with prospective partners. It didn't matter if you were dating or not. As far as most Nigerians were concerned, single was single until married.

Her mind went back to Daniel, and how she still

hadn't heard from him. Steeling herself, she dialled his number. There was no point just sitting around waiting, when she could reach out to him.

The phone rang on his end, but he didn't pick up. A little deflated, she considered letting it go until whenever he decided to call, but after a few seconds, she typed out a quick text.

Hey...Just checking to see how you're doing. Take care. Hope.

There was no reply. She closed her eyes and took a deep breath, then set the phone down and forced her mind to focus on other things.

Like Agnes, who was at her desk, staring silently at her blank computer screen.

Hope chuckled. "Don't tell me you're sleeping with your eyes open."

Agnes slowly swivelled her chair. "I'm not sleeping," she mumbled. "Just thinking."

Her eyes were red-rimmed and shiny with tears. "Are you all right?" Hope asked, alarmed.

Agnes shook her head. "I'm so not."

"Are you ill? I can drive you home if you want."

"No. I'm not ill."

Hope pushed her chair closer to Agnes. "Do you want to tell me about it?"

"I need to talk to someone," Agnes sniffed.

"Seriously. Or else I'll start to think I'm going mad, or that there's something wrong with me."

Hope looked around the office. It was almost lunchtime. She thought quickly, trying to come up with a convenient and private place where Agnes would be comfortable talking.

"You know what? I'll order snacks so we don't have to go out for lunch, then we can go to one of the conference rooms and talk."

Agnes agreed. Hope sent out the order on her phone then led the way to the smallest of the conference rooms.

Inside, it was quiet. Hope left the lights off and the shutters drawn, then drew out a chair for Agnes. "Tell me what happened."

Agnes sniffed. "You know I started seeing someone some time ago, and after we hooked up, he just...he didn't call me again."

The *full package* guy. Hope remembered. "But you said you'd moved on to someone else."

"Yes," Agnes confirmed. "The thing is...there was this other guy. I met him here, though we didn't really talk...I'm sure I told you about him...one day when I was going on about a cute guy I saw in the office...with lips like sugar?" She gave Hope a questioning look. "Do you remember?"

Something like dread unfurled in Hope's stomach. Silently, she nodded.

"He only said hi that day," Agnes continued, "and he gave me his card. Then I saw him again at Greg's house..."

Charles, Hope thought. It had to be Charles. "The baby's dedication party."

Agnes nodded. "We flirted a bit at the party, but I still didn't call him, though I thought he was gorgeous. Then, after Bayo never called me back...I finally called him. I just wanted to do something fun, to help me forget, you know?"

Hope could only nod, hating the direction the story was going.

"His name is Charles, by the way," Agnes said. Her face had a faraway look for a moment, as if she was still remembering Charles with longing and pleasure. The look was quickly replaced with one of hurt. "I called him. It was a weekday, I remember. We talked...he was in a meeting, but he told me to come over to his office and I went...waited for him, then we went to his place."

She looked at Hope, who was trying her best to keep her face expressionless. "I think he had to discharge some other girl...but I wasn't surprised. Hot guys like that...there's always a girl, you know?"

Hope nodded. "I know." And she knew, without

a doubt, that she was the girl he'd had to discharge. He'd kept her waiting for hours, without bothering to call and cancel, because he'd found someone else willing to give him the sex he wanted without *needing time* or being fussy about a past relationship with him.

"Anyway," Agnes continued. "I just wanted to feel attractive after being dumped. It's not as if I wanted anything from him."

"I understand," Hope said with a sigh. Inside, she was raging. She couldn't believe that even for a moment she'd thought maybe Charles had changed, that maybe he deserved another chance. Just from Agnes's face, she already knew where the story was going. Charles had hurt Agnes, somehow. With him, a woman always ended up hurt and broken.

"After that, I saw him a few times," Agnes was saying. "It was just a casual thing. I know his type of guy. I knew he probably had other girls, but I'd been to his house and there was no sign at all that he was married."

There were voices and footsteps as someone walked past the outside of the conference room. Hope closed her eyes, dreading the part of the story she knew would come next.

"So, what happened?"

Agnes let out a long shuddering breath. "About a

week ago, he stopped taking me to his house. I didn't think anything about it. I just thought...change of scenery you know? Then last night, we went to this guest house here in Victoria Island. He booked this luxury room for a night, but he said he had to leave around eleven because one of his younger siblings was visiting and he didn't want her spending the night alone at his place..."

Another lie, Hope thought wryly. Charles didn't have any younger siblings.

"Anyway, that's how we ordered room service o and when they brought the order, two babes followed the waiter inside the room." She paused. "Hope, one of them was his wife. Can you imagine! His wife! She rained insults on the both of us. She took pictures. I felt so ashamed. She called me a prostitute, told me to test myself for STDs. She said some things to him too, accused him of sleeping around when she was outside the country having their baby. Then her friend threw me out. I had to put on my clothes in the corridor and find my way home by myself at that time of the night."

Hope cursed Charles silently, watching as Agnes shuddered at the remembered humiliation. She put her arm around Agnes. "Sweetie, I'm so sorry, but it wasn't your fault. He didn't tell you he was married."

"But I feel so..." Agnes shook her head. "Am I

cursed? Why do I always attract the demons? I feel
so humiliated, seriously. I never want to see another
man again for as long as I live."

"You're not cursed. I wish I had known you were
seeing him. I'd have told you...I know him from way
back, Agnes, and he's a liar, and an asshole. He's the
one who cheated on his wife. You didn't know, so
you did nothing wrong."

Agnes looked uncertain. Hope patted her back,
thinking how easy it would have been for her to be in
the same situation. It could have been her, caught in
an intimate position with Charles. It could have been
her at that hotel.

He said his wife left, but he omitted to say she
left temporarily to have a baby abroad.

And she'd almost believed him.

She'd almost let him back into her life.

And if she had, she would be the one crying now,
dealing with the humiliation of being disgraced by
his wife.

She wished she had the opportunity to tell him
what a lowlife he was, to tell his wife what a worm
she was married to. Memories of all the pain he'd
caused her through the years flooded her mind, and
it took all her self-control just to focus on Agnes.

She comforted her friend, and by the time they
returned to their desks, Agnes was looking slightly

better than before. "You deserve better," Hope told her, "And you'll find someone much better, I promise."

Agnes shrugged noncommittally and reached for the snacks Hope had ordered earlier, which were now cold. She ate, looking morose as she went back to staring at her screen.

At least the heartbreak hadn't affected her appetite, Hope thought. With any luck, the pain wouldn't last too long, and she would get over Charles and the humiliation he never failed to serve to the women who made the mistake of falling for him.

CHAPTER THIRTEEN

AGNES WENT HOME EARLY, pleading a headache. Hope watched her leave, wishing someone would teach Charles a lesson.

There was a beep from her phone, and she picked it up, releasing a breath as she tried to calm her thoughts. Hoping it was a text from Daniel, she was disappointed to see it was just an advertisement from a local supermarket.

He still hadn't responded to her message.

What if he never replied? What if he decided that he wasn't willing to wait for any girl?

She closed her eyes, then shrugged. Well, it would be his loss. If a little hesitation was too much for him, then maybe he was just like Charles, looking for eager girls to use and discard.

The thought made her feel guilty, because she knew that he was not like Charles at all.

When her phone rang again just before she left the office in the evening, she was shutting down her computer and putting on her shoes at the same time, so she answered it without looking at the screen.

She almost melted when Daniel's warm voice filled her ears.

"Look who forgot about me," he teased.

"I so didn't forget about you," Hope protested, almost ashamed of the flood of relief she felt. "*You* forgot about me."

"I did?"

"You did. At least, I tried to reach you today. I even sent you a text."

"And I'm calling you right now."

She rolled her eyes. "So why didn't you call me before? All week."

"I've been in a crazy situation, meetings all morning, product surveys all afternoon, and meetings in the evening too. I've been in Beijing all week and I feel as if I've been in a prison camp.

"Oh," Hope was surprised. "I didn't know you weren't in the country."

He sighed. "I'd been putting the trip off for a while, then it rushed up on me this past Monday with a vengeance. I had to go."

"But you're back now."

"Just landed."

"Hmm." He'd called her as soon as he landed. Pleasure fanned in her belly. Then she reminded herself that he'd gone a week without speaking to her. "I just wanted to check on you earlier. I noticed I hadn't seen you around, and I didn't know you travelled, so."

"I guessed."

She heard him say something to someone, probably one of his staff, then he came back on the line. "Hope…" He paused and his voice was gentle. "I wanted to call, many times."

She nodded, feeling silly when she remembered he couldn't see her. She understood from his tone why he hadn't called. She'd told him she needed time, and he'd given her the space she needed to decide if she was ready.

"I'd like to see you," he said.

"I'd like that too."

She heard someone on the other end talking to him. He responded to the person. Then he was talking with her again. "I'll call you."

He didn't say when. "Okay," Hope said, wondering if she should be worried about that. "I'm glad you're back, Daniel."

Late in the afternoon, the next day, she finally

saw his name light up her screen. She reached for the phone, eager to hear his voice.

Calm down, Hope. Calm down. You don't even know where this thing with him will go.

But it was too easy to ignore that sensible inner voice once Daniel said her name.

"Hope." As always, he said it like he loved the way it sounded on his lips.

Hope expelled a tense breath. "Hi."

"I just woke up." He laughed. "I think I slept for fifteen hours straight. It was great to be home in my bed again. I was exhausted, then ravenous. Where are you?"

"I'm home," Hope replied, yawning.

"Are you still in bed?"

"Hmm mmm," Hope replied unselfconsciously. "I got back into bed after breakfast. I was tired from a hard week at work, you know?"

"Exhausted from missing me, you mean."

She chuckled. "Well, there was a bit of that too."

She heard him breathe. "I want to see you," he said. "What are you doing this evening?"

She almost said she wasn't doing anything, then she remembered Ebisan's party and groaned internally.

"I'm attending a birthday party for one of my friend's husbands."

"I resent them already for taking you away from me, even for just one evening." Daniel laughed. "Where's the party?"

"On the island." She described the location.

"Oookay," he said. "I'm just going to do some work over here, since you're too busy for me. I may surprise you later though—maybe show up there before you leave."

"That's mildly stalker-ish," Hope said, laughing.

"Is it?" He seemed surprised. "Well, I probably will. Unless you tell me specifically not to."

"I'm not doing that. Your mild stalker-ishness is fine with me."

"That's a relief." He chuckled. "So, I'll probably see you later, okay?"

"Okay."

She got ready for the party and was already on her way downstairs when she remembered that Ebisan planned to introduce her to some guy. It was amusing. The last thing she needed was yet another guy.

As she drove towards the island, she imagined what scenario would be at the party. As eager as she was to see Ebisan and catch up, she wasn't keen on being surrounded by smug married couples talking about marriage and parenthood and giving her pitying looks for not being able to relate. Everybody would have one eye on her and Dennis, wondering and calculating whether their meeting would lead to something serious.

Hope rolled her eyes at the idea. She hoped Daniel would come and rescue her before it got too weird, awkward or boring.

She got to the restaurant and parked, turning off her car radio, which had been blasting out loud alternative rock. She noticed her phone was ringing, and as she picked it up, it stopped. The screen showed three missed calls.

From Charles.

Hope shook her head. Nope. Not today.

The ringing started again. As she stared at the screen, tempted to ignore the call, she remembered Agnes, and anger won over restraint.

She touched the screen. "Hello," she said, her voice dripping with disgust.

"Hi." Charles's voice was soft. "Hope," he sighed. "How are you?"

Perfect without you, scum! Mentally, she kicked herself for still feeling anything, even resentment. "I'm fine," she replied evenly. "Why are you calling me?"

"Come on," he cajoled. "Don't be like this."

"Like what?"

"Angry."

Hope laughed. She wanted, more than anything, to make him feel like he was nothing. "Why are you calling me?"

"I wanted to explain about the other night."

"What night?"

"Hope." He drew out her name. "I want to explain why I didn't show up."

"Oh...that night. The one where you hooked up with one of my colleagues? My friend?" Hope shook her head. "No need to explain. I already know you're trash."

He was quiet.

"Are you surprised that I found out? Have you explained to your wife what you were doing in a hotel with another woman? Does your wife know you're going around Lagos telling women she left you? Congratulations on your baby, by the way, since that detail wasn't important enough for you to mention."

"You're angry," he said calmly, after a pause. "and I understand. I can explain."

Hope listened, her irritation increasing with every word he said. "I'm not interested."

"Hope." His voice turned into a coaxing purr that increased her irritation. "It's more complicated than you think. I want us to talk. Let's talk, please."

"About what, Charles?" Hope snapped. "Talk

about what? How unreliable you are? How you've always lied to me? Deceived me?"

"See, this is why we need to talk," he said softly. "I can't let you just...carry all that anger around."

Hope was quiet. Somewhere inside, she was starting to suspect that she was just entertainment to him. This thing he was doing—trying to make her emotional, trying to twist her around and resurrect her pain...it now seemed like he was just bored and using her for trips.

"Where are you?" he asked suddenly, changing tack.

"I'm at a birthday party," Hope replied

"Tunde's party?"

Hope sighed. "Yes, Tunde's party." She'd forgotten that Charles also knew Tunde and Ebisan from back in school. The thought that he would be at the party increased her irritation.

"Okay. Don't worry. I wasn't invited. Tunde found out about the surprise and told me. His wife can't stand me, so I didn't get an invitation."

"How sad for you," Hope muttered, sarcasm dripping from her voice.

"Let's do it like this," Charles said. "I'll come over and explain things to you."

She knew what he was doing. She had been angry with him many times before, but that anger never survived being face to face with him. That was why she had cut off all communication when he got married.

Did he still think just showing up would put her at his mercy again?

If he did, then he was in for a surprise, because she would not hesitate to show him how little he meant to her.

"Do whatever you want," she said with disinterest. "I have to go now. I don't want the party to start without me."

She knew he would come, and it wasn't until she got out of her car she remembered that Daniel planned to show up too.

Hopefully, she'd dismiss Charles with a tongue-lashing he would never forget, long before Daniel arrived.

She left the car, going into the restaurant to find Ebisan, Tunde and a few other guests who had arrived and had clustered around a table on the popular back terrace overlooking the ocean. After a few enthusiastic hugs and greetings, and an introduction to Dennis, a handsome guy who seemed only cursorily interested in Hope, she settled at the table.

There was food, lots of drinks and laughter, and a delicious cake that melted in Hope's mouth. One by one, the guests gave toasts. Dennis was beside her, but they didn't talk much until after the cake had been cut and he finally remembered that he was meant to be her pseudo-date for the evening.

"Ebisan was telling me she introduced us before," he said.

Hope nodded. "That's what she said...At their wedding. A long time ago."

He smiled. "I can't believe we didn't hit it off." He paused. "So, she tells me you're an engineer." He wiggled his eyebrows. "Wow!"

"Why *wow*?"

"I don't know." He laughed. "It's such a male-oriented course."

Hope smiled. "Male-oriented? People still say that?"

He looked puzzled. "I mean, men are more interested in areas like engineering, or architecture... just saying. Women usually go for banking, insurance, sometimes Law...though..." he shrugged, and she surmised that even that one was something he considered male-oriented too.

"Well, I am interested in engineering. What does that mean for your generalisation?"

He smiled. "That you're one in a million?"

Hope shook her head. "Now you're trying to parlay what you said into a compliment. I think I know exactly why we didn't hit it off the last time Ebisan introduced us," she smiled, then turned to the person seated on her other side, who, luckily, was another girl she'd known back in school, ignoring him until he got the message.

Her phone buzzed not long after. Charles again.

"Do you want me to walk into the party and give them something to gossip about, or will you come outside to talk to me?" he said silkily.

"Are you threatening me?" Hope snorted. "I'm sure your wife would like to hear that you gate-crashed a party to talk to an old girlfriend."

"You're not that old," he said.

"You're not funny."

He sighed. "Come out, babe."

The endearment annoyed her, giving her the surge of emotion to stalk outside to give him a piece of her mind. If he wanted a tongue-lashing, then she would give him one.

She found him standing outside, on one side of the main entrance doors of the restaurant, overlooking the carpark. He was leaning on a brick wall, his arms casually folded over his chest.

"Where are your wife and her friend hiding," Hope mocked. "When do they plan to burst out with cameras and insults?"

"Leave my wife out of this," Charles

murmured, his voice even and pleasant. He uncoiled himself from the wall, but Hope was too annoyed to notice the grace in his movements, or the beauty of his spotless white caftan. She wouldn't have cared anyway, as far as she was concerned, she was finally and irrevocably done with him.

"You should have left her out of it," Hope said. "*My wife left,*" she mimicked his voice. "You have no shame."

He peered at her, a curious frown on his face. "Why are you so angry?"

"You don't know?" She threw her hands up. "You're the single biggest mistake I've ever made in my life. You stole my innocence. You stole my illusions. You're a cheat."

He shrugged nonchalantly. "I'm still the best thing that ever happened to you."

Hope laughed. "No, Charles. You're trash." She paused. "You know...The only reason I came out here was to say that to your face. You are trash. I know you're trash. Agnes knows you're trash. Your wife knows you're trash. Every woman you ever touch finds out eventually that you're trash. Soon even you won't be able to hide from the knowledge that you are trash."

It felt good to say, and her satisfaction increased

even more when the smile fell off his smirking lips, and his eyes narrowed with something like anger.

He didn't enjoy having a mirror held up to his behaviour? Well, that was his business.

A movement caught her eyes, and she saw a familiar black SUV drive into the parking lot, from the distance she couldn't tell if it was Daniel's, but as it inched forward, coming to park close to where she and Charles were standing, she knew instinctively that it was him.

"Do you feel good now? After you've said all that? Are you satisfied? Is this where you wait for me to beg for forgiveness so you can feel righteous when you take me back?"

Hope stared at Charles nonplussed. "You think I still want you."

"Oh, Hope...I remember you used to say that a lot. You'd claim you'd never forgive me, then after I told you what you wanted to hear, you couldn't wait to drag me into bed." He smirked. "Do you blame me for missing how eager you always were? How responsive? How needy?"

Memories and humiliation flooded her mind. "You're living in the past. I'm not that girl anymore."

His response was a mocking chuckle. "You are, and if I hadn't let you go that night at my place.

You'd be addicted to me again, begging me to give your body what we both know it wants."

He knew. He knew that if he'd insisted that night. She'd have given in to him, and lost in the pleasure he could give her, she might have forgiven anything, even his lies.

"Why not accept it?" he drawled, watching her as her composure slipped. "You know you can't walk away from us."

His voice was soft, but the expression in his eyes was almost malevolent. She closed her eyes as realisation flooded her. "You don't care about anyone," she hissed. "Not me, not anyone else. I've always been just a game to you."

He snorted dismissively. "You loved getting played."

Anger rose, and disgust, for him, for herself. "You are a bastard," she flung the words at him, then turned on her heel, but he gripped her arm, stopping her.

"Stop pretending." he said. There was something venomous in his voice. "What are you going to do? Hold on to your righteous anger forever? I dumped you once, so what? It didn't stop you from dropping everything to run after me just because I paid a little attention to you. Admit it, you're lonely and desperate and I'm doing you a favour even wanting to sleep with you."

His grip on her arm was like iron. Alarm, panic and utter humiliation flooded her and tears welled up in her eyes. Then she was free, and she saw that Daniel was standing between them. She thought she heard a punch, but she was too humiliated to find out. Without waiting to see what was happening, she hurried back inside the restaurant.

The party was still going on, and she retrieved her purse, saying a hasty goodbye to a concerned Ebisan before going back outside.

She walked past Daniel, who was waiting for her at the reception. She didn't say a word to him as she hurried through the doors towards the parking lot. Outside, to her relief, Charles was nowhere to be seen, but she heard Daniel's steps behind her.

"Hope." She heard his voice just as she unlocked the car.

She almost burst into tears. She was humiliated that he had witnessed that scene with Charles. She wished she had any excuse to be angry with him, so she wouldn't have to explain Charles and why she'd been talking with him in the first place.

Suddenly feeling weak, she leaned on the car door, and when Daniel came up behind her and put his arms around her, she didn't say a word. She allowed herself the safety she felt in his arms. After a while, she turned around to face him, her eyes still wet with tears. He reached into his pocket to retrieve a handkerchief, slowly dabbing her eyes and cheeks.

"It's all right," he whispered. "I'm here now."

CHAPTER FOURTEEN

DANIEL HELD her for a long time, his fingers gently stroking her back. Hope relaxed into his arms, allowing his gentleness to calm her raging and confused emotions.

In his arms, she felt appreciated...and loved.

The realisation was too much, too soon. She pulled back from him and his hands slid away from her body. She drew in a sharp breath, feeling the loss of his touch.

"Are you all right?" His voice was soft as he peered at her.

Hope nodded, then laughed weakly. "I'm fine. I'm fine...I have no idea why I was even crying."

He nodded, then opened her car door and motioned for her get in. She obeyed and waited while he rounded the car and joined her inside. He sat beside her, studying her face.

"You're sure you're fine?"

She nodded and handed him his handkerchief. He folded it and slid it into his pocket.

"Do you want to tell me about it?"

There was concern in his eyes, and curiosity too. Understandably, he wanted to know who Charles was, not just as someone who cared, but as someone who was interested in her.

She couldn't blame him. Of course, he would want to know who and what stood in his way, if anything.

"He...Charles..." Hope let out a long breath, hating that the conversation was necessary. "We used to go out when we were in school. He got married...and I didn't see him for a while, then I ran into him recently."

"He's the ghost from the past, the one who kept you waiting that night at the office." There was a pause. "He's also the guy you were with...at that party...a couple of weekends ago."

Hope swallowed the faint humiliation that came with the memories, focusing instead on the gentle tone of Daniel's voice. "Yes. That's him."

Daniel nodded. "Go on."

"I haven't spoken to him in a while...since that

night at the office anyway...then he called me on my way over here and when I told him where I was, he came over, said he wanted to talk...and he said some nasty things, which, I guess I needed to hear."

"I doubt there was anything he had to say that you needed to hear," Daniel said dismissively.

Hope shuddered, remembering the malevolence she'd heard in Charles's words, and the humiliation she'd felt. "I know," she agreed softly. "I just...feel like a fool for thinking...for ever thinking there was something worthwhile in him."

"You're not a fool," Daniel said.

"Thanks."

Daniel's eyes lingered on her face. He patted her hand but said nothing. His silence was slightly unnerving. Hope tried to imagine how the scene with Charles would have looked to him. She remembered his face all those weeks ago at the Leton party? Was he judging her again? The thought caused a twinge of pain in her chest.

She watched silently as he drew his hand back from hers and tapped a short rhythm on the top of his thighs. "He's the reason you wanted to take it slow?"

Hope sighed. "Not because I still thought I had feelings for him or anything. I just needed a little time alone before...moving into something with someone else."

"I understand," Daniel said. "I'm...I shouldn't even be asking that now, while you're upset. I just wanted to be sure who he was."

"He's no one."

Daniel shrugged. "Are you okay to drive?" The concern was back on his face, but Hope didn't want concern. Not if it looked like Charles would remain a shadow between them.

"Don't change the subject," she said. "Tell me what you think. You don't believe me when I say he's no one? You think I'm probably still in love with him or something?"

He studied her face, his expression inscrutable. "This is the wrong time to talk about this," he said.

"It's not the wrong time if you're thinking it," Hope shot back. She was angry and there was an illogical desire to let that anger out. "I have an ex-boyfriend who's an asshole. He invites me on dates then leaves me stranded. He is rude and threatening to me in public. He lied about being separated from the wife he dumped me for. He also slept with my colleague on the same day he stood me up." She sucked in a breath. "Is that too messy for you? Are you going to judge me the way you did when you saw me at that silly party?"

"Don't be ridiculous," Daniel snapped.

Suddenly, tears were stinging at her eyes. It felt like he was pulling away, and she didn't know how to draw him back. There was a strange desperation welling up inside her, making her want to say things she knew she would regret later, making her want to put him on the defensive, even though he had done nothing to deserve it.

He's not Charles, she reminded herself. The last thing she wanted to do was repeat the old patterns that had come from trying to manage a bad relationship for years.

Daniel sighed, and when he spoke, his tone was gentle again. "Is it so surprising that I'm concerned about your relationship with this guy who keeps popping up around you?" he said. "I want you, Hope, but I'm not willing to share your emotions."

She folded her arms. "I'm not asking you to do that."

He chuckled. "Hope, I don't think your life is too messy. Nothing involving you would ever be too messy for me."

The stinging in her eyes intensified. "Daniel..."

"No, wait..." He stopped her. "I got jealous when I saw you at the Leton party with him, especially since you shut me down when I tried to ask you out earlier. My ego was bruised, and I didn't want to risk another rejection, so I decided to leave you alone."

"So, you snubbed me at the office."

"I did," Daniel said, nodding slowly. "I was trying to forget about you."

"It really hurt," Hope murmured, remembering. "I wasn't sure why it hurt so much at the time, but it did."

There was a teasing glint in his eyes. "Are you sure now?"

Hope gave him a look. There was a lot to the question. Was she sure how she felt about him now? Did she still want to wait?

"I think I am."

They were both quiet. Then Daniel smiled at her, before glancing around the car park. "You want to go back into the party?" he asked. "Looks like it's still going on. I haven't seen any crowds of people leaving yet."

Hope shook her head. "I'm not in the mood for any more partying, plus...they set me up with some guy who thinks women shouldn't study engineering."

Daniel laughed out loud. "He sounds like a strong masculine type. I think you should go back inside, give him a chance at least."

She stuck out her tongue. "Nah...I don't think so."

"So...should I take you home, or..." he looked at her.

"Or...what?"

"We could go to my place."

She swallowed, searching his face for any sign that the invitation meant anything more than what it seemed on the surface. "Yes, why not?"

Daniel drove, with his driver trailing them in Hope's car. Their destination was in Banana island, on a quiet street with new houses and paved sidewalks shaded by blossom covered trees. He approached a tall black gate, and it slid open electronically to reveal a compact two-storey home, set far back from the fence. He parked in an open garage which housed three other tarp-covered cars.

"Here we are," he said, turning to Hope.

"Here we are," she repeated, trying to calm the wisps of nervous expectation unfurling in her belly. She climbed out of the car and smiled when Daniel came to her side and took her hand.

"You have a nice house," she told him.

"One of my few indulgences." There was a faint hint of pride in his voice. "Though, I don't spend as much time here as I should."

"Workaholic," Hope teased.

"You've joined them," he laughed, leading her to the entrance and letting her precede him into the foyer. Inside, it was bright and cool, and the décor looked like it was professionally done.

"Do you want anything?" he asked, once they were inside the living room. "Food...something to drink?"

"I already ate at the party," Hope said, shaking her head. "You?"

"Yeah, I had something before I came to find you."

"So..." She went toward the sofa and drew her fingers over the plush leather. "What are your plans for me?"

Daniel's grin was wolfish. "Nothing much. We can watch some TV, maybe a movie, then I'll show you around the house."

"Perfect," Hope said. "Very PG. I like."

He looked amused. "I'm not always PG."

Something in the quiet words caused a clenching in her lower belly. "Umm." Her mouth suddenly felt dry. "I wouldn't expect you to be."

He chuckled before disappearing for a few moments in the direction of the kitchen. He returned with microwaved popcorn and drinks, and they watched a movie. After that, he showed her around the house, and Hope was surprised to see that even though it looked compact from the outside, it was spacious.

"I'm loving your décor," she told him. Each room was furnished tastefully but there was nothing ostentatious. On the walls, there was an interesting mixture of local and foreign art. Obviously, he was something of a collector.

They ended up on the balcony, where there was a stunning view of the ocean and a huge lounge chair from which they could enjoy the view together. Hope nestled in his arms, drowsy and comfortable.

She dozed off, and when she opened her eyes a while later, Daniel's arms were still around her, but his eyes were closed, and he was breathing deeply.

The balcony was lit only by dim ceiling lights, but they were bright enough for her to make out his features. She studied his face, the strong planes and angles, the carved beauty of his nose and lips... Staring at him, she itched to stroke every inch of his skin, to feel his lips...

He opened his eyes and caught her devouring him with hers. "You see something you like?" he teased.

Hope laughed self-consciously and wrinkled her nose. "Yeah, a little."

"Only a little?" Daniel groaned. "I'm hurt."

Hope giggled. "Okay...maybe a lot."

She watched him laugh, wanting nothing more

than to stay in that moment, with him, for as long as possible.

"How long was I asleep?" he asked.

"I don't know," Hope stretched. "I just woke up myself."

His eyes lingered on her body, then he glanced at his watch. "It's getting late."

Hope groaned. "Don't remind me. I don't want to get up from here."

She felt him move, turning his body, so he was facing her, resting on one elbow. He traced the line of her chin with one finger, and she lay there, feeling the warmth radiating from his body and getting almost breathless with anticipation.

His eyes met hers. "I'm going to kiss you," he murmured.

Hope felt her entire body tremble, but she didn't say a word. The next moment, he leaned down and his lips covered hers. Hope moaned at the contact, a delicious feeling of pleasure spreading all over her. His hand was splayed over her stomach, his fingers flexing idly as his lips explored hers.

His hand moved, curving around her waist and hovering at the top of her hip. She pressed closer to him, craving the feeling of his hard body against hers, then, still kissing her, he rolled her on top of him, so she was lying on his chest.

He released her lips and placed his hands beneath his head as he gazed up at her.

"I don't know if I prefer kissing you or looking at you from this position," he said.

Hope folded her arms on his chest. "I think I prefer kissing you."

He grinned. "I'm all yours."

She placed a quick kiss on his lips, almost shyly. "Why is your chest so hard? Why are you so fit? You're making me self-conscious."

"I work out every morning for an hour. I use the time to think." He shrugged. "...and I can assure you, you have nothing to be self-conscious about."

She closed her eyes, enjoying the sensation of lying on his body, being so close to him. She lingered there until she started to feel drowsy again.

"I should go home," she said. "I don't want to."

"Don't encourage me," Daniel warned. "The slightest excuse and I'll keep you here for as long as possible."

Hope's closed her eyes at the image. "That sounds tempting."

He laughed. "Come on, I'll drive you."

Hope got to her feet. "I can drive myself, you know? You don't have to drive me home with your driver trailing behind in my car."

He looked at her as if she was speaking a strange

language. "That's an extra half hour I get to spend with you. You can drive if you like, but I'm coming along."

Hope laughed, her insides unfurling with happiness and pleasure. He took her hand, and they went downstairs.

She drove her car, while he stretched out in the passenger seat, fiddling with her radio. His driver followed behind to take him back home. When they got to her house, she parked on the street and they kissed again, then she watched as he walked over to his own car.

Excitement and fulfilment mingled in her stomach. He waved, and she waved back. He climbed into his car and remained there until Ayuba opened the gates and she drove into the compound.

She floated up the stairs to her room, her body still flushed with pleasure as she prepared to sleep. Just as she climbed into bed, her phone vibrated. It was a message from Daniel.

"I definitely prefer kissing you too."

Hope grinned. She was still on a cloud of pleasure when she fell asleep.

CHAPTER FIFTEEN

"This one you're always on the phone nowadays," Hope's mother said one evening as Hope walked into the house, her phone at her ear. Daniel had left the country on a short business trip, but they spoke every day, sometimes late into the night. Hope didn't mind, she would have sacrificed every wink of sleep just to keep hearing his voice.

"Talk later," Hope said to Daniel, ending the call before turning a brilliant smile in her mother's direction. "Good evening, mama mia."

"Hmm. Who are you talking to that you're smiling like this?"

"You don't know him," Hope replied, giving her mother a quick hug before running up the stairs.

Her mother followed. "Him? And you're just

going? You won't tell me anything? Grace has already given me some details o."

Hope stopped walking and turned back to face her mother, imagining different methods to wreak revenge on her sister for betraying her trust. "What did Grace tell you?"

Her mother shrugged. "Nothing serious, just that you were interested in someone..."

"Why did she tell you?" Hope moaned. Now her mother would start planning weddings and marrying her off prematurely.

"Why won't she tell me? Anyway, I can see by the way you've been smiling up and down that she's right."

"Ohhhhh!" Hope groaned, going to her room. She just wanted time to get to know the guy. The last thing she needed was someone feeding ideas into her head.

Not that she minded the outcome her mother was anticipating. Daniel was great...He was handsome, funny, attractive, sexy...he was also, rich, very rich, and eligible. There were probably other girls misinterpreting anything he said to them, hoping that he meant more or wanted more.

She didn't want to set her heart on him and end up feeling rejected or discarded.

But she was falling for him. In fact, she had gone past falling, and it made her both fearful and excited.

THERE WAS a lot to do at work that week, and by Friday, Hope was suffering from both mental and physical exhaustion and couldn't wait for Daniel to return.

She was dying to see him. They'd been chatting nonstop all day, and around closing time, she got another message from him.

When are you leaving?

Soon.

Okay. Can you do me a favour.

Anything.

thinking face Anything?

smiley face Just tell me what you want.

She was still waiting for a reply when her phone rang.

"I got a delivery at my office," Daniel said, his deep voice warming her down to her toes. "and I was wondering if you could pick it up for me. I'll get it from your house tomorrow, since I have zero intention of coming near the office at all this weekend."

Hope wondered why he didn't just get one of his

staff to take it over to his house, but she was sure he had his reasons. "No problem. I'll go up and pick it up on my way out."

"My assistant will meet you at the reception, okay? So, you don't get lost."

She rolled her eyes. "Hilarious."

When she was ready, she freshened her make-up and went out to the lobby, then took the lift to the floor that housed the main entry to the offices of Daltech Information Systems, Daniel's company. She approached the glass reception desk, where a pleasant-faced receptionist was already smiling at her, but before she got there the main glass doors leading into the office slid open and a guy appeared. He was dressed in a well-tailored suit, and he made directly for Hope.

"Hope?"

"Yes."

"I'm Tobi, Daniel's assistant. He asked me to wait for you. Just follow me, I'll take you to his office."

Hope allowed him to lead her. Through a glass partition, she could see a lot of workspaces, and she wondered how many people Daniel employed. Tobi led her to a small branched-off lobby, where a single elevator waited. He pressed the call button and soon they were on their way up.

The lift opened into the penthouse floor, into a small reception where the girl at the desk waved them through. Beyond that was a large office, with about four people seated at their desks. At the far end of the office, a pair of frosted glass doors led to, what she guessed, was Daniel's office.

She wondered why he hadn't just asked Tobi to give her the package—whatever it was—at the reception, but she was curious to see where he worked, so she didn't mind. Tobi opened the frosted glass doors and stood back to let her through.

She stepped in, awed by the spacious office, the large desk, the plush arrangement of furniture, the large screen opposite the desk that showed a blow-up of some computer program, the spectacular view of the lagoon, and more than anything else, Daniel, standing by the wall to wall glass windows, smiling at her and looking very pleased with himself.

"You're back," Hope hurried toward him, unable to stop herself. He closed the distance quickly with his long legs, and soon she was in his arms, in a sweet hug that felt just right—as if their bodies were made to fit into each other. "Why didn't you tell me you were here?"

"I wanted to surprise you." He gave her a mischievous wink. "Seems I succeeded."

"You did," Hope laughed, almost giddy with happiness. "It's so great to see you."

His chest rose, and he hugged her closer, then, holding her hand, he moved back towards the desk and perched lightly on the edge.

"I missed you," he said, relieving her of her bag and setting it behind him on the desk.

Hope smiled. "I missed you too, but why aren't you at home, resting or something."

"I had a few things to check on, and..." He looked at her. "I wanted to see you."

A rush of pleasure suffused her body. "Well, now you have seen me," she said. "I hope you're pleased."

His eyes glinted. "Very pleased."

The way he said the words made her stomach flip. She was standing in front of him, close enough to feel the hard strength of his body. She swallowed.

He took a deep breath and closed his eyes. She could feel his exhaustion, and she wanted to put her arms around him. She could already imagine it, his head resting on her chest, the spice of his cologne in her nose...

She took a breath to steady herself. "Your office is fantastic, very impressive."

He opened his eyes. "Thank you. I'm glad you like it."

"You must be so tired," Hope continued,

thinking of his long flight. She touched his cheek, her fingers lingering. "Have you had anything to eat?"

"Just before you came. What I need now is sleep. My driver is waiting to take me home." He smiled wryly. "I just don't want to leave you yet."

"You're making me feel very special." Hope said.

Daniel held her gaze. "Then I'm doing something right."

She sighed, wanting nothing more than to melt into him. "Go home and get some rest. And then tomorrow, you can spend the whole day making me feel special." She leaned forward and kissed him on the lips, and his hands encircled her waist, pulling her closer and deepening the kiss. Pleasure flooded her, pleasure and desire. When he released her, they were panting softly.

"Hope." Her name was a soft whisper on his lips.

She closed her eyes and swallowed. "Yes."

"You're driving me crazy." He took her hand in his and kissed it gently, then rose from the desk. "Come on," he said. "I'll walk with you to your car."

He held her hand all the way down to the car park. At her car, he kissed her again. "Tomorrow," he murmured, and there was a promise in the words.

Hope nodded. "I can't wait."

THE NEXT DAY, she was awake early, surprising her mother by going downstairs to help with the Saturday chores.

"Are you sure you don't need to rest," her mother asked as Hope dusted and arranged shelves in the kitchen. "I know how hard you work and how tired you must be."

Hope shook her head. "I have excess energy this morning."

Truth was, she was excited. She'd spent the entire night gorging on the memory of the kisses she'd shared with Daniel and looking forward to seeing him again.

After all the chores were done, she went to take a shower. When she came back downstairs, her father was in the living room.

"Are you going out?" he asked.

She nodded.

"I guessed as much." He chuckled. "I know it's not the thought of spending the day with me and your mother that has you looking so excited."

Hope laughed. "But daddy, I like staying at home with you guys."

"Don't like it too much," he cautioned, his eyes twinkling. "Your mother and I are already talking about evicting you so we can enjoy our old age."

After breakfast, she went upstairs to change.

She'd already set out her clothes for the day, a light green dress in loose jersey fabric with a belt at the waist, and jewelled wedges that showed off her glossy red pedicure. As she contemplated the outfit, her phone rang.

"When should I come to pick you up," Daniel said. He sounded well-rested and full of energy.

"You're already awake?" Hope asked, "I expected you to sleep for longer."

He chuckled. "I'd rather see you."

She smiled. "Okayyy...Now I'm blushing all over the place."

"Are you?" She could almost hear the smile in his voice. "I would love to see that."

"I'm sure you can make me blush when we're face to face."

"I intend to."

She pulled in a breath. "You can start coming now. I'll be ready in about half an hour."

By the time she finished dressing, Daniel still hadn't called her to tell her he had arrived, and she wondered if there was traffic. Deciding he would only be a few minutes at the most, she slid on her shoes and went downstairs.

At the head of the stairs, she was startled to hear his voice in the living room.

She stopped walking, not sure how she felt about

this latest development. She hadn't planned for him to meet her parents yet and she wasn't sure she was ready.

Inside the living room, she saw Daniel on one sofa, looking at ease as he answered a question her father asked. They were talking about data storage technology, and he was explaining some detail to her father, who looked very interested. Her mother, perched on her favourite seat, was assessing him covertly with an expression of approval.

"Hello," Hope paused at the archway leading into the living room. She turned a puzzled glance towards Daniel. "I thought you would call to tell me when you got here."

"I was just about to send Justina to get you. Your friend is telling us about his company," her mother said, sounding too pleased for Hope's liking. She could almost hear the wedding bells clanging inside her head.

"I'm ready," she said pointedly, looking at Daniel. He smiled and rose, making a quick small bow as he extended a hand towards her father, then her mother. "It was nice meeting you sir, madam."

They said goodbye, and she waved awkwardly at her parents before following Daniel to where he had parked inside the compound.

"I didn't hear you drive in," she said. "I didn't know you planned to come inside."

He shrugged. "The gateman opened the gates as soon as he saw my car, so I drove in. It seemed rude to be in the compound and not come inside to say hello to your parents." He unlocked the car and opened the passenger door. "Did you not want me to meet them?"

"No, that's not it. I just..." She paused, searching for words. "It's kind of early for you to be getting the boyfriend interrogation."

He looked nonplussed, then laughed, joining her inside the car. "I didn't get the *boyfriend interrogation,* whatever that is. Your parents couldn't have been nicer."

"Hmmm."

He chuckled. "Don't you think I can handle a few questions from your parents?"

"I know you can." The thing was...It wasn't him she was worried about.

It was herself.

She didn't want her parents to decide that they liked him, when she wasn't even sure exactly where they were going with their relationship.

And if things didn't work out, she didn't want questions or disappointment from her family to compound the disappointment she'd already be feeling.

He put on the radio while he drove. It was tuned to a local radio station, and as the hosts talked and made jokes, she listened with half an ear, silently watching Daniel, the way his fingers played with the wheel, the angle of his jaw, the way his body seemed to lounge even as he drove.

His eyes skipped to her, and he raised a brow. "What are you thinking?"

"Nothing," Hope replied.

"You were looking at me for so long and thinking nothing?" He looked disappointed. "Maybe I need to work on my game."

Hope laughed. "Your game is perfect."

He grinned and one hand left the wheel to squeeze hers, just for one sweet moment, then it was gone. "I knew I was doing something right," he said.

Yes, you are, Hope thought. You're doing everything right.

CHAPTER SIXTEEN

THE NEXT MONDAY, Hope spent most of the morning in meetings, but listening to the senior partners nit-picking over design issues, projects, and deadlines couldn't dispel the haze of happiness whenever her thoughts strayed to Daniel.

Around her wrist was a stunning watch with a slim face encrusted with gleaming stones. A gift from him. It was one of the most beautiful watches she'd ever owned.

"Nice watch," Agnes observed, when she returned to her desk after the meeting.

Hope gave the watch another loving glance. "Yeah, I know. Thank you."

"You're just glowing anyhow."

"Am I?"

"Yes. *Man* kind of glowing."

Hope guffawed. "That's different from ordinary glowing?"

Agnes nodded. "Yes now. Anyway," She lowered her voice. "Someone was telling me she saw you and Daniel Amadi over the weekend." She gave Hope a measuring look. "When are you going to tell me what's up?"

"I don't know what's up for sure yet," she said with a small, dismissive wave of her hand. There was a part of her that wanted to hold everything about Daniel close to her heart, as if sharing what was happening between them would diminish it somehow. "We went out a few times."

Agnes raised her brows. "Girl...you have to play your cards right o! You know he's a catch."

"I like him," Hope said. "I don't care about him being a catch or whatever. I just really like him."

"Don't fall in love too quickly though. This one you're *liking* him. With these men, it always pays to guard your heart. Don't just love blindly. Think ahead. Plot your moves. Make sure that emotionally you're the one on top." She stopped and laughed. "I don't know why I'm telling you all this. Me that as soon as a guy smiles at me, I forget myself."

Hope chuckled. "It's not like I even know how to plot my moves in the first place." And, if it was a matter of falling too fast, the warning was far too late.

She had already fallen for Daniel. She was at that point where losing him would hurt, really hurt.

"How about you," She asked Agnes, changing the subject, "You're no longer dwelling on that other thing, are you?"

A deep sadness entered the other girl's face and Hope cursed Charles silently.

"I'm trying not to," Agnes said.

———

Daniel had called earlier to ask her to join him for lunch, so at noon, Hope went to his office.

He was at his desk, but rose as soon as she entered, walking over to pull her in for a hug before stepping back to look her over. "You look beautiful."

"I look stressed," Hope replied. "I've been in meetings all day.

"Me too, but you still look prettier than me." He ran his hands down her arms and she sighed. When he got to her hands, he threaded his fingers with hers and lifted them up to his lips, then grinned when he saw she was wearing the watch. "Do you like it?"

"Are you kidding? I love it."

"I'm learning your tastes," he said proudly, leading her to the seating area, where two plush leather sofas surrounded a low glass table. "I've already ordered lunch. Jollof rice."

"Ah!" Hope giggled. "Our national pride."

They were talking about the merits of Jollof versus fried rice when there was a knock and his assistant opened the door, letting a uniformed catering staff into the office. The guy disappeared after setting the food on the table and receiving his tip. As Daniel opened the dishes, Hope realised how hungry she was. There was Jollof, fried chicken, plantains, and fresh juice, and it was delicious.

Later, her hunger quenched, Hope went over to the windows to admire the stunning view of water glistening in the afternoon sun. From the distance, it was impossible to see the debris and pollution that was obvious when you saw the lagoon waters up close. From the height and distance, it just looked beautiful.

She felt Daniel come up behind her, felt his body as he stood inches from her. She closed her eyes, her breath quickening as she waited for him to say something, do something.

His hands touched her nape, and she shivered when he moved her hair aside and laid a soft kiss on her neck. He was driving her crazy, and she was sure he knew it. She wanted to turn around and throw all caution to the wind, discard any doubts and surrender to the pleasure she knew he could give her.

She sighed and leaned closer to him. He let the kiss linger then straightened and came to stand beside her.

"It's a nice view," Hope said, her voice breathy.

Daniel smiled. "Funny, I was thinking the same thing just a few moments ago."

"Oh." She frowned, then chuckled. "I'm glad you liked what you saw."

His smile was crooked and amused. How could she ever have thought he wasn't her type? He was everything, and her heart fluttered at the possibility of him as wholly and totally hers. He was nothing like Charles. She knew that now. He was a man who could be trusted.

"Don't think about him." Daniel's voice roused her from her thoughts.

How had he known what she was thinking? "I...Daniel..."

He shook his head. "I know you, Hope. I know you're thinking about work when you have that small frown in the middle of your forehead and your fingers start tapping. I know what you look like when you're hungry. And when I see that mixture of confusion and regret on your face, I know who you're thinking about."

His eyes were level with hers. He wasn't looking for reassurance, just telling her how well he knew her.

"My regret isn't that I can't be with him. It's that I ever was."

Daniel's lips moved in a wry half-smile. "It's ultimately up to you, but I don't want you to think of him, whether with disdain, hate, resentment, or regret. Not when you're with me."

Hope nodded slowly.

His eyes traced her features. "I am possessive, Hope." The words were quiet. "I won't share any part of you. Not even your thoughts."

There was no space for anyone else, not when she wanted him more than she'd ever wanted anything, or anyone else.

"I'm not playing around with you," he continued. "I'm not a guy who likes to waste my time. I'm here with you right now, because this is where I want to be, and you're who I want to be with. I want to know that you feel the same way."

Hope swallowed. "I'm not playing around either." She placed a hand on his arm. "This is where I want to be."

He pulled her into his arms, sealing the words with a kiss that left her breathless. She melted against him, wishing she didn't have to return to her office.

On the way back to her floor, she wondered what the conversation meant for their relationship. As conversations about commitment went, they had clarified nothing for sure. Were they dating? Exclusive? Serious?

She wasn't sure.

Well, whatever they were, she decided, for now, she was happy. Too happy to waste any time on something as useless as worrying.

FOR THE NEXT FEW DAYS, they spent as much time together as work permitted. They both had a busy week, so when Daniel suggested a weekend getaway, Hope was more than willing.

"Just your passport," he said when she asked him what she needed to bring, but on Thursday night, she packed a weekend bag with a few clothes, swimwear, and lingerie.

On Friday morning, Mr Samson, Daniel's driver came over to the house to pick her up. Daniel was already in the office tying up loose ends so he could be free from work all weekend.

He was also busy all day, so there was no chance

to see each other. Hope had a lot of work to get through too. She worked late into the evening, while trying not to be distracted by the ball of excitement in her belly just waiting to explode. After most people had left for the day, she saw Daniel's name flashing on her phone.

"Ready?" he asked without preamble.

"Sure. You?"

Daniel laughed softly. "Honey, I've been ready all week."

Almost shaking with anticipation, she hurried to meet him on the ground floor. He took her hand in his but waited until they were in the back seat of his car to pull her into his arms for a long lingering kiss.

"I've been thinking of doing that all day," Daniel said later.

In response, she kissed him again. He smelled like heaven and tasted even better. Overwhelmed by her physical desire for him, she wanted nothing more than to keep touching, tasting...to be as close to him as possible.

He drew her onto his lap, his strong hands sending sparks of pleasure through her body wherever he touched. When he finally released her, her eyes were unfocused.

He grinned, his eyes dancing as he gazed at her. "I should steal you away more often," he said.

She settled into his arms. "I wouldn't mind." She wouldn't mind being stolen away anytime he wanted.

The driver headed toward the airport, going to one of the charter companies where, on the tarmac, a plane was waiting. Their destination was a popular tourist resort off the east coast of Africa. She'd never been there but knew enough to expect beautiful beaches and delicious seafood.

"We'll be flying all night," Daniel said after the smooth take-off. He sat opposite her, so she could devour him with her eyes without having to crane her neck. He had undone the first two buttons of his shirt, and her fingers itched to finish the job.

"All night?" She smiled at him. "How do you plan to entertain me?"

He chuckled. "With food."

She made a face, and he laughed. "You don't want to eat?"

I want to look at you, Hope thought. "I don't mind."

"I'll probably doze off at some point," he said, smiling apologetically. "I'm already trying not to succumb to exhaustion."

Meanwhile, she was trying hard not to tear his clothes off. Hope smiled, amused at the thought. "Don't worry about me. Sleep if you want to."

A hostess came in with drinks on a tray, then disappeared and returned with chocolates, cookies and fruit. Daniel popped a candied date into his mouth. "These are good," he said.

"Have you been there before? Where we're going?" Hope asked, mildly curious. She only knew he travelled a lot for work.

He nodded. "A few times."

Hope gave him a sidelong glance. "Alone?"

He grinned and lounged back in his seat. "Are you asking me if I've ever been there...with another girl?"

"No! I mean...I...Yes, I guess. Have you been there with another girl?"

He laughed. "And if I have, you'd be jealous?"

Hope made a face. "Maybe. Yes?" She sighed. "Now you probably think I'm unreasonably jealous and possessive."

He shook his head. "Hope, I'm jealous of every man you've ever smiled at." His voice was light and playful. "Now, that's weird."

"No, it's not." Hope was smiling. "It's kind of endearing."

He smiled. "I haven't been here with another girl," he added seriously "I don't have a habit of flying girls out of the country for weekends of debauchery."

Weekends of debauchery. Hope bit her lower lip and met his gaze from under lowered lashes. "Is that what this is? A weekend of debauchery?"

He replied with an unreadable smile and popped another date in his mouth. "Enjoy your feast," he said, the smile still playing on his lips. "I'm going to sleep for a while."

Hope slept too, and when she woke up, the sky outside was lightening to grey. Daniel was awake and looking at her, a tender expression on his face.

"Hey, you," she murmured.

"Hey you," he replied.

She stretched. "How much longer?"

"About an hour." He got up and came to sit beside her. "You look beautiful when you sleep."

"I don't snore and drool?"

"I noticed nothing like that."

Hope smiled. "Like you would tell me."

They talked for a little while, then as their destination approached, took turns to freshen up in the bathroom before landing. The journey through the airport was a breeze and before long, they were in a hired car heading for their hotel.

Exhaustion had set in again after the flight, so Hope didn't pay attention during the check-in at the hotel. They were staying in a beautiful cabin right on the beach, and even in the morning light, Hope could see how lovely it was, especially with the soothing sounds of the ocean surf.

One of the hotel personnel brought their luggage to the cabin then left them alone.

"Do you like it," Daniel asked, busying himself with transferring their bags to the closet.

"I love it," Hope exclaimed.

"Why don't you take a shower while I order breakfast," he said, smiling. "I'm ravenous."

Hope was hungry too. She went to the bathroom and after a warm, relaxing shower changed into a comfortable tank top and loose lounge shorts. Since they were both tired from the flight, they were probably not going to go out all morning, so there was no point in dressing up just yet.

While they waited for breakfast, Daniel took a shower too. He emerged just as the food arrived, wearing a ribbed vest over grey sweatpants.

Hope caught herself staring and closed her mouth. The combination of grey sweatpants and Daniel's ridiculous sexiness was enough temptation to make her want to slobber all over him. Even the room service attendant wasn't immune, staring at Daniel with open appreciation.

He was perfect.

And he was hers.

The thought made her want to purr like a kitten.

They ate the feast of French toast, eggs, pancakes, coffee and fresh orange juice. By the time she was full, her eyes were drooping.

"You should get some sleep," Daniel said, noticing. "In the afternoon, we can explore the beach."

"You don't mind?"

"Why would I?" he patted her knee. "I don't want you staggering around exhausted instead of enjoying yourself."

Hope didn't need any further urging. She burrowed into the softness of the king-sized bed and in seconds, she was fast asleep.

When she opened her eyes, Daniel was in bed with her, asleep and breathing deeply. Her gaze landed first on his broad chest, then his gorgeous face. She'd always thought it was a cliché in novels when women *couldn't help noticing* how boyish men looked while sleeping, but it was true. He looked sweet and innocent.

She touched a finger to his lips, smiling when they twitched. She shifted closer to him, turning so her back touched his chest. He brought his arm over her belly and pulled her into his body, making her sigh. She felt safe and comfortable in his arms, and she almost drifted off to sleep again.

"Do you want to start exploring now," he asked, his voice rough with sleep.

She could think of a lot of things she wanted to explore. "Yes," she replied breathily.

He turned her around, so they were face to face, then nipped gently at her lips before kissing her fully. Hope moaned, flames of desire licking at her insides. When he released her, she was panting softly.

"I meant the beach," Daniel said, smiling innocently.

"I don't care what you meant," Hope said, reaching for him again.

This time, he let the kiss last for a few moments longer, before lifting her off the bed and setting her on her feet.

"Let's go outside," he said with a gentle smile. "I don't want you to spend the whole trip indoors."

Hope made a face. If it meant satisfaction for the raging need inside her, she didn't mind staying inside all week, all year even. He was torturing her by making her wait, and Hope was sure he knew it.

Resisting the urge to kiss him again, she got dressed. He didn't do things lightly. She knew that. So, if he was hesitating, he probably had a good reason. But what could it be?

They walked on the beach, then basked in the sun, before having lunch in one of the cool lounges in the hotel. In the evening, they went to the town and visited a few shops before visiting an impressive restaurant for dinner, then they returned to their room, where they shared sweet, lingering kisses, and an exhausted sleep.

For the next day, Daniel had booked a couple's massage, and after that, it was more of the same–the beach, food and the most relaxing experience Hope had enjoyed since she could remember.

"I could do this every weekend," she told Daniel, when it was time to leave. She felt as if every cell in her body was rested and relaxed. "I could do this every day, in fact."

He was on the bed, watching her zip her luggage. "Stick with me," he replied with a wink. "You know I can make it happen."

Hope went over to him, pulling him up from the bed so they were standing facing each other. "I wish we had more time," she whispered, meeting his eyes. "I wish..."

He lowered his head and kissed her. Hope moaned. Being around him all weekend had felt like slow ignition, and her body was at a fever pitch. She wrapped her hands around the back of his neck, her eyes closing as her body melted into his. The naked hunger and desire in his kiss demanded a response that came from deep within her body. She wanted everything. She wanted to give him everything.

Daniel's chest rose as he pulled back. "I want to devour you," he murmured. It wasn't an invitation or a proposal. It was just a statement of fact.

Hope breathed. She could feel the tension in his muscles. She could feel the wild thudding of his heart, and she felt him, pressed against her, the unmistakable evidence of how much he wanted her. It made her almost unwilling to let go of him, even for a moment.

"But...?" Hope held his gaze.

Daniel smiled. "Patience is a virtue?"

"Right now, it really doesn't feel that way."

He lowered his head again, kissing her forehead, then the tip of her nose. He kissed the corner of her lips, then trailed soft kisses to the spot beneath her ear. She moaned.

"I want a lot more from you than sex," he said in a gentle, mesmerising voice. One hand trailed down her back and over her hips, leaving a trail of pleasure and desire.

"I already know that," Hope breathed.

He chuckled softly and kissed her again. "I want to know that you're ready, Hope."

Was he hesitating because he thought she still

had doubts? She took his face in her hands and met his gaze squarely. "I've been ready forever."

His eyes flared, but he said nothing. He lowered his lips to hers and she surrendered to him. It took a while to hear the knock on the door, and when he finally released her, Hope was unsteady on her feet.

Their car was ready, and even though Hope wanted nothing more than to shut the outside world away for a few more hours at least, they were soon on their way back to the airport.

They talked for most of the flight back to Lagos, seated side by side. Desire lingered, just under the surface, and as they held hands across the seats, Hope felt as if he was already making love to her, only with words instead of his body.

She dozed off in the car on the way to his house, only awakening just as they entered the gates. Mr Samson took their things upstairs, while Daniel's cook laid out a light dinner on the balcony. After they ate, there was a sudden power cut, and soon after, the hum of power generators filled the air.

"Lagos," Hope said with a chuckle. She was standing at the balustrade looking out at the evening view. Water and lights. Behind her, Daniel remained seated, watching her.

"But you missed it," he said.

"I did." She laughed. "It's not my fault. We all have a love-hate relationship with this city."

He stood, and Hope's heart thudded as he walked over to join her, each step determined. He stood close beside her, and wordlessly, she turned to face him. In the next moment, she was in his arms, kissing again, hungry and desperate with a desire that had banked steadily until it finally burst into flame.

"Don't stop," she whispered, when his lips trailed to her neck. *Don't ever stop,* she added silently. Her heart felt tender and full, and fervent desire swelled in her belly. His hands on her body were igniting her skin. He pressed her body flush against him, and she heard herself moan.

He pulled away, and she reached for him, unwilling to stop.

"Hope," his voice was rough.

She swallowed. "Yes..."

"If I don't let you go now, I won't let you go tonight."

The words were supposed to make her think, make her consider leaving, but they only took the flames of her desire and turned them into a raging explosion of need.

"I don't intend to go anywhere," she replied, meeting his gaze.

She expected him to kiss her again, but he didn't, instead he lifted her in his arms as if she weighed nothing, then he was carrying her away from the balcony, through a short hallway, and into his bedroom.

He laid her gently on the bed, and covered her body with his, leaning his weight on his elbow as he devoured her mouth.

"Hope," he said it, at some point, the way he always did, as if her name on his lips was something that brought him pleasure. She responded by drawing his lips down to cover hers again.

Being with him was a feast of the senses. Every touch, every taste, was a new, intensely pleasurable experience. She surrendered to him, revelling in the feel of his beautiful, powerful male body. He explored her with his hands, his lips, his tongue, and she'd never wanted anything the way she wanted him.

When he finally surged into her, the pleasure was indescribable. Her body tightened and exploded and still he was there, perfection personified, his every movement designed to fill her with helpless pleasure. He gave her his strength and his love and every inch he had to give, pushing her over the precipice of mindless ecstasy.

Later, she lay with her head on his chest while he

stroked her hair. There was no sound except for the low hum from the cooling vent.

"What are you thinking?" he asked.

Hope smiled and looked at him. "How happy I am."

He rolled her onto her back. "You know," he said with a grin, hovering over her. "I still have a lot of happiness to give."

Hope lifted her head and kissed him. "What are you waiting for?" she breathed.

He covered her mouth with his, and they didn't talk much for the rest of the night.

CHAPTER SEVENTEEN

HER WHOLE BODY WAS TINGLING. Hope stretched and opened her eyes, her lips curving at the memories from the night before. She reached for Daniel, but his side of the bed was empty.

She drew herself up just as he entered the bedroom from the walk-in closet. Hope pulled in a breath. He had already dressed for work in a charcoal suit that made her want to drag him back into the bed.

"Hey." Her voice was soft, almost shy.

"You're awake." He came over to the bed and placed a tender kiss on her lips. She was wearing one of his t-shirts, one she'd found in the closet when she visited the bathroom in the night. It was much too big for her, but she loved it.

"This suits you," Daniel said with a smile, fingering the hem.

She laughed. "I wish you didn't have to go to work. You could have done like me and taken the day off."

He kissed her again. "I'm the boss. When I take a day off, everybody takes a day off, and the world descends into chaos."

She giggled at the melodrama, then sighed. "I had a great time."

"Will you be here when I get back?" He sounded hopeful.

Hope hesitated. She'd planned to leave in the afternoon, to go home and get ready for work the next day, but... "I'll stay if you want me to."

He grinned. "I want you to. I'll take you home when I get back, okay?"

"Okay." Her fingers found his tie, and she caressed the soft silk, then pulled him down for another kiss. "I'll be waiting," she promised.

She spent the day happily doing nothing. There were a few calls from the office to clarify project issues, but aside from that, all she did was lounge around the house, explore, and enjoy the exquisite meals Daniel's cook served for breakfast and lunch. She watched a few movies and read a book on her phone while waiting for him to return.

He finally did, early in the evening. Hope was out on the balcony and didn't hear him drive in, which intensified her happy surprise when he walked out to join her. She barely held back from launching herself into his arms like an excited child.

"You're back early," she said, going to him. He had taken off his jacket, leaving only the tailored shirt. She ran her fingers over the crisp material, breathing in his spicy cologne.

"I couldn't wait to see you." He smiled. "I had to exercise a lot of self-control or I would have returned earlier, but...the wait was worth it. Coming home to you is like living in a fantasy."

Hope blushed. "You should have returned as soon as it crossed your mind. I wish you didn't have so much self-control."

He chuckled. "Trust me, I'm barely holding on to it." He lifted her into his arms, and she wrapped her legs around him, holding on as he carried her to his bedroom.

It was a few hours later before they drove over to the mainland. As the car idled in front of her house, Hope did her best to staunch the intense desire to stay with him—to prevent the magical weekend from ending, and it seemed like he felt the same way. He held her hand in his, his fingers stroking hers.

"I don't want to go inside," Hope whispered.

"We could go back to my place." Daniel met her gaze, and she knew he was serious.

She laughed. "It's like you want my parents to disown me." She'd told her mother she was travelling out of the country for a weekend of rest, but she hadn't offered details and surprisingly, her mother hadn't asked, except to say Hope was to let her know when she arrived at her destination and make sure her sister knew where she was and with whom.

"They won't disown you," Daniel said, kissing her palm. "They know you're in good hands. I passed the *boyfriend interrogation*."

Hope smiled. "I miss you already," she whispered.

He kissed her again, then squeezed her hand. "I feel the same way."

THE DAYS that followed were pure bliss. Almost daily, they had lunch at his office, or somewhere close on the Island, and in the evenings, after work, they ended up at his place for a few hours alone before Hope had to return home for the night.

He stopped by Grace's house one Sunday to watch the football match with her brother-in-law and Gerald. He took Hope to meet his older sister Stephanie and her family. Hope warmed to the tiny woman, who looked nothing like Daniel, but was obviously very close to him.

She teased him mercilessly while Daniel feigned outrage. Her children, excited at seeing their favourite uncle, climbed all over him after opening the treats he'd bought for them.

"I hope he's treating you well," She told Hope. "If he does anyhow, let me know. I won't pity him."

Hope laughed. "I know he won't do anyhow."

"You're right," Stephanie agreed. "He's one of the good ones."

The more Hope got to know him, the more perfect he seemed. She wanted to be careful, to guard her heart, but there was a part of her that realised she was already too far gone.

"Auntie Hope, do you have a boyfriend?" Her niece, Diana, was tugging at her hand. It was a Sunday, and Grace had arrived with her whole family to spend the day with the proud grandparents.

Hope looked up from her phone, where she'd been reading a message from Daniel. "What did you say?" she asked, half amused and half incredulous.

"Mummy said you have a boyfriend. Grandma said that's why you're pressing your phone."

Hope stared at her niece. "They said all that. Hmm. Well. I have many friends that are boys."

Diana looked unimpressed. "But do you have a best friend that is a boy?"

"Diana, leave Hope alone o," Grace said from across the living room.

"You're the one telling everybody that I have a boyfriend," Hope said with pursed lips, as Diana, bored with the whole conversation, ran up the stairs to join her younger siblings.

Grace was laughing. "As if anybody needs to tell anybody. You have romance written all over you."

Hope tried and failed to stop herself from smiling.

"See?" Grace exclaimed. "We should find time to talk though, so you can update me."

"We really should," Hope agreed. There was a lot to tell. "But not today. I'm abandoning you guys. Daniel is coming to pick me up."

"Love is sweet o."

"Did I hear that you're going out?" Their mother came into the living room from the front porch where her husband and son-in-law were enjoying the cool weather outside with glasses of cold drinks.

"Yup," Hope said, getting up. "He'll be here any minute, so I'm going upstairs to freshen up."

Patience gave her a side-eye. "It's not by all these going out going out o. Tell him to bring wine, so we know which direction we're going."

Hope ran up the stairs. "I can't hear you."

She heard her sister laughing behind her. "I like this one," she heard Grace say. "Not like that Charles."

Her mother snorted. "Don't even mention that name in my house. We met Daniel. Your father and me. He's very well brought up and responsible..."

The rest of the conversation faded as they went to join the men outside.

Hope continued to her room and quickly changed into a pretty dress and sandals, applying a little makeup, before heading back downstairs. Now, at this point in their relationship, it felt good that her family liked Daniel.

It felt like they were on the threshold of something more serious.

And she didn't mind that. She didn't mind it at all.

Daniel had told her he was close, but as the children, tired of playing with their nanny and Justina, ran down the stairs with her, she heard his voice mingling with the other voices out on the porch.

So, he had already arrived. Her heart kicked. It was silly, crazy even, that no matter how much time they spent together, the excitement she felt at seeing him never diminished. She opened the door to the porch and stepped out with her escort of noisy children, and found Daniel with her family, enjoying a chilled glass of palm wine.

She halted at the door as the children ran out to beg for sips of palm wine. Daniel had been saying something, and now he stopped talking and their eyes met.

It was almost painful, the intensity of all the things she felt when she looked at him. He was a thousand times more than she had ever thought it was possible for a man to be. He was everything she hadn't even known to hope for, or to want.

"Hello," she breathed.

"Hi." He rose to his feet, his gaze appreciative. He wore a simple white native attire, and the only thing preventing her from walking into his arms and claiming a kiss was the crowd of family looking at them with unveiled interest. "I got here a couple of minutes ago. I was just waiting for you."

"Yeah...I heard your voice from inside."

"We're still here o," Grace quipped, her amused

voice finally causing Hope to tear her eyes from Daniel's.

"Sit. Finish your wine," Hope's father added. Daniel lowered himself back on his chair, smiling.

"Auntie Hope, so that is your boyfriend," Diana observed archly, causing one of her younger brothers to giggle.

Grace gave her daughter a stern look.

"What?" Diana complained, rolling her eyes.

The adults laughed. Daniel finished his drink and rose again, saying his goodbyes before leading Hope to his car.

"You look great," he told her, once they were inside.

"I know."

He laughed. "My mum has been asking when I'm bringing you over to see them."

"Really?" Hope had met Daniel's mother when the older woman showed up at her son's house unexpectedly on a Saturday. Hope and Daniel had, fortunately, only been watching a movie. She'd fussed over Hope and invited her to come to the family house.

"Yup. And now my dad has joined the chorus." He smiled at her. "I don't know...it seems they're getting the idea from somewhere that I'm really really serious about you."

Hope bit her lip. "I wonder how come."

Daniel laughed. "I've never been able to hide my obsessions from my parents."

Obsession. Hope met his gaze before he turned his eyes back to the road. In a way, the word mirrored her feelings towards him.

She was obsessed with him, and that realisation came with its own fears.

"How many other obsessions have there been," She asked, almost ashamed at the faint licks of jealousy at the thought of any other women who had come before her.

He laughed. "Are you asking me about my body count?"

"Well..."

"It's not a lot," he said, sounding amused. "You don't have to be scared that I've been a raging womaniser or anything like that."

"I wasn't thinking you were a raging womaniser."

"So what were you thinking?"

Hope sighed. "I was just a little jealous. It's stupid. Forget I said anything."

His eyes were serious when he looked at her again. They were at a red light, and he placed one hand on her arm and squeezed it lightly. "When it comes to you and me, Hope," he said quietly. "You have absolutely nothing to worry about."

THEIR DESTINATION WAS a lounge inside VI. The cool interior was spacious and smelled of cocktails and finger foods. On one wall, a huge TV showed a football match that seemed to interest only a few people, possibly a rerun or one of the lower clubs.

At the bar, a bored looking barman wiped glasses and took orders, and a group of five, three guys and two women, stood around the pool table, watching as two of the guys played a game.

As soon as Hope and Daniel entered the group at the table turned to greet them.

"Daniel!" The tall dark guy holding a pool cue came over and gave Daniel a short hug, before holding out his hand to Hope.

"Hope, finally. I'm Briggs," he announced, pulling her into a bear hug.

"Briggs has been following me around since secondary school. I don't know what to do about him," Daniel said, laughing as he introduced his friend.

"It's nice to meet you," Hope said, immediately liking Brigg's friendly persona.

Daniel introduced her to all the others. There was Uche and his beautiful wife Ceecee who was visibly pregnant, and Temi and her fiancé Deinde.

"I hope Daniel is not trying to pretend that he's someone who likes to relax and hang out o," Temi told Hope. "Your bobo likes to work."

"I know," Hope replied. "He's admitted that he's a bit of a workaholic."

"A bit?" The other woman laughed. "I pray."

"Stop spoiling my market," Daniel told his friend. "Hope works hard too, so we're a perfect match."

"Awww," Briggs brought his hand to his heart, then twirled the cue stick. "Who else wants to challenge the god of snooker?"

The rest of the evening was boisterous and fun. After a few hours, everyone started to go home. Hope, Daniel, Uche and Ceecee, were the last to leave, and when they reached the car park, they stood around Uche's car saying their goodbyes when another car drove in.

Hope didn't register that the car looked familiar until the passenger door opened and Agnes stepped out in a short dress and high heels. She looked beautiful, and her face was wreathed in smiles.

"Agnes," Hope started to call out, then stopped when she realised who Agnes was with.

Charles.

He stepped out of the driver's side, just as Agnes saw Hope and beamed, hurrying over to give her a hug. Charles watched Hope with a mocking smile, enjoying her confusion.

"Hope!" Agnes sounded blissful. She gave Hope a quick hug. "And Daniel Amadi..." She wiggled her eyebrows at Hope and held out her hand to shake Daniel's.

Hope wasn't sure what to say or do. Daniel made quick introductions, while she stood looking at Agnes and wondering if her friend had gone mad.

"I didn't know you guys were here," Agnes was saying. "You should meet Charles..." She turned back towards the spot where Charles had parked and saw that he had walked on ahead of her to the entrance of the lounge. He stood there waiting, looking smug, impatient, and distant.

"What are you doing?" Hope asked.

"Saying hi to you." Agnes replied with a nonchalant shrug. "...and enjoying my weekend."

Hope took her hand and drew her out of earshot of Daniel and his friends. "What are you doing here, with him?"

Agnes shrugged again, but her eyes lit up. "We made up," she said. "He explained everything. Hope, I think this one might really be serious. He was miserable without me. He cried and begged me to..."

Hope had heard enough. "You are too brilliant to believe this kind of nonsense," she snapped. "He has shown you exactly what he is. Why are you being foolish?"

"Why are you being insulting?" Agnes countered. "I know you said you knew him..."

"Know him," Hope laughed bitterly. Angry at Charles, and at Agnes for being stupid. "That person you're with...he broke my heart and almost destroyed me. Whatever he's doing with you...he's doing it to get to me."

Agnes face turned cold. "I know you like to feel superior, Hope, but it's really thoughtless of you to imply that a guy can't be interested in me unless he's trying to make you jealous."

"Thoughtless?" Hope shook her head. "Agnes, you're making a mistake..."

"No, I'm not," Agnes retorted, her voice rising.

Hope stopped talking, taken aback by her friend's tone. She watched as Agnes walked away, toward the entrance, towards Charles, whose smirk in Hope's direction said he knew exactly what they'd been talking about.

Agnes climbed the steps in her heels, and Charles put his arms around her, his eyes meeting Hope's again just before he lowered his head to kiss Agnes on the lips.

CHAPTER EIGHTEEN

By the time Hope returned to where Daniel was standing, Uche and Ceecee were already driving off. She waved lamely at the retreating car while Daniel stood tall and silent beside her.

"Are you ready to leave?" he asked, an odd coldness in his voice.

Hope nodded, not really taking note. All she could see was the smug look on Charles face, the knowing smile before he kissed Agnes. He was trying to get to her.

She seethed silently while Daniel unlocked his car, still quiet. She fiddled with her phone, her mind churning. She wished she could go back in there and drag Agnes away from Charles before he hurt her again. Her friend was trusting, but she didn't deserve to be lied to, to be a pawn in Charles games...

The journey to Daniel's house passed in a blur. How could Agnes be so foolish, so willing to dismiss all the red lights and dive headlong into whatever Charles was promising?

She heard Daniel toss his car keys on a side table and she smiled in his direction, still distracted. He didn't smile back.

"I have some work to do," he said quietly, heading toward his study.

"Work?" It was the first thing she'd said to him since they left the lounge. "Now?"

He stopped and smiled. There was no humour in the expression. "Your mind is obviously occupied with something else."

Hope sighed. "I'm so sorry, I was just thinking about..."

"I don't care," he interrupted. "I have work to do, Hope. If you'd rather go back to the lounge and finish your showdown with your ex and his new girlfriend..." he gestured toward his car keys. "Feel free."

Hope stared at him. A part of her knew that she was feeling too much, reacting too much to seeing Charles with Agnes, but another part of her bristled at Daniel's dismissive tone.

"What are you talking about?" She asked.

His expression was cold. "I'm too busy to waste

my time on something I can't have," he said. He started to walk away, then stopped. "It only took seeing him with another woman for you to forget that you were with me. What did you have to say to Agnes that couldn't wait until later? Were you so eager to stake your claim and let her know he was off limits?"

She was already angry, with Agnes, with Charles, adding Daniel to the list was only too easy and despite her better judgement, she did exactly that. "For God's sake! Was I supposed to just...watch my friend get swept away by a man I know to be a player?"

"Were you concerned that he's playing your friend, or reacting because he's still playing you?"

She took a deep breath, turning away from his penetrating gaze. "He's not playing me."

"Isn't he?"

"No." She said the word, but knew that she was lying, to him, to herself. Charles had changed the course of her evening, changed her emotions and her state of mind, just by showing up.

She turned imploring eyes at Daniel, but she could feel her connection with him slipping away, almost as if right there and then, he was putting up a wall between them.

"As I said," he continued with a dismissive shrug.

"If that's where your heart is...I would just rather be doing something else with my time."

He wasn't only talking about his work now, Hope realised. He was talking about them. If she wasn't fully committed to him, then he would rather not be with her.

She stared at his back as he walked away, her earlier anger had given way to dread...because she knew she couldn't bear to lose him, especially not over someone like Charles.

He was walking toward his study, and she followed him inside the thickly carpeted room furnished with a desk and large bookshelves. He stopped at the desk and turned to see her standing at the door. His eyebrow rose in a silent question, as if he had already sent her on her way and was wondering why she was still around.

The careless dismissal was rankling.

"Stop overreacting, Daniel. Agnes is my friend. I had to warn her about Charles."

His eyes narrowed at the mention of Charles's name. "Did you? Right then and there? You had to walk away from me? You couldn't wait? You were willing to risk making a scene because of *him*?"

Somewhere in the back of her head, she knew she could have waited. She knew she could have spoken to Agnes later. But she saw Charles's smirk in her head, and it made her lose her ability to stay calm.

"I didn't make a scene. Stop making me have to defend myself for being concerned for my friend."

"I'm not making you do anything," Daniel said with a shrug. "You are absolutely free to do whatever you want and go wherever you want."

"Then stop using that dismissive tone with me." She took the few steps to the desk, facing him squarely. "This is unnecessary. You're letting your unwarranted jealousy ruin our night..."

"Unwarranted?" His laugh was harsh. "Jesus, Hope...It's unwarranted for me to be jealous when just the sight of your ex with another woman makes you forget where you are and who you're with? Look how angry you are, because of *him*."

"Because he hurt me."

"Of course. How can I forget, when obviously, you will never let it go?"

"I have let it go," Hope said. "I have let him go."

Daniel shrugged.

That dismissal again. Her temper rose. "Maybe it's not me who's still holding on to him," she snapped. "Maybe it's you. You're so jealous of a shadow from my past, you see a simple conversation as disloyalty."

His only response was a shrug.

Hope wanted to stamp her foot. "I didn't know that being with the *almighty* Daniel Amadi was a situation that prohibits conversation with anybody else. I guess I know that now."

His eyes flared, but he said nothing. She wished he would say something. Anything. His silence felt more condemnatory than words.

"You're seriously asking me to leave?"

He shrugged. "This argument is obviously not the optimal use of my time."

"Screw you and the optimal use of your time," Hope burst out, her eyes stinging. "Jesus, Daniel. You're so full of yourself that it's astounding that you can even be jealous of a godforsaken louse like Charles. You're so convinced that you're better than everyone else, but you're not."

He remained silent. Cold and unyielding, like a block of ice. It scared her to see him like that. It scared her to think she could lose him, just like that.

"What happened to all the..." She swallowed. "You said you wanted to be with me, and now you're just going to send me on my way like a badly prepared meal because I *reacted* to seeing my ex with my friend?"

She stared at his expressionless face and took a deep breath. "You know what? You don't deserve me. I hope your self-righteousness keeps you warm tonight, Daniel. I'd rather be alone than be with a sanctimonious perfectionist like you."

She'd barely turned around when he rounded the desk to block her way. He towered over her, so she had to tilt her head up to meet his burning eyes.

"First of all, I don't appreciate being told that I'm full of myself and self-righteous. Second, I remember telling you very clearly that I won't share you, not your body, not your thoughts, and definitely not your heart."

"And now you don't have to, because I'm leaving."

He moved forward, crowding her into the desk. "No, you're not."

Something in his tone made her heart start to pound. "Don't tell me what to do, Daniel. Have fun being perfect after I'm gone."

He chuckled, then cupped her chin and tilted her face up to his. "You're not going anywhere."

She was still standing with her back to his desk. Her fingers curved around the thick edge. His forceful tone, his touch...her anger...everything had somehow coalesced into an unbearable tension low in her belly. "You asked me to leave," she breathed.

"And then you insulted me, accused me of *unwarranted jealousy*, questioned my motivations..." He paused, his flawless face just inches from hers.

"After all that," he mused. "How can I just let you go?"

Hope shivered. She was still angry, but her body wasn't sure whether it was in a quarrel or about to be seduced. There was barely an inch between them, and she could feel the barely leashed fury emanating from him. Still, she didn't back down. "You were the one who chose not to have a conversation," she challenged.

"You want us to have a conversation? About your reaction to your ex?" His eyes darkened. "Okay, Hope. Let's have a conversation."

She opened her mouth to respond, but something in his eyes made her forget just what she planned to say. She held up her hand, touching his chest just as his lips closed over hers. Her emotions were rolling and chaotic, and she was sure he was angry, but his lips were gentle on hers, the kiss, a slow burning tease that ignited a raging fire deep inside her.

Was this punishment? Affection? Love? She didn't care anymore. She forgot about Charles and Agnes. She forgot her anger at Daniel's cold dismissal as her body softened and begged for more.

His hand cupped the back of her neck, holding her head in a firm but gentle grip while his mouth touched, tasted, claimed...driving her mad with need.

Her senses went into overdrive. Her hands slid over his chest, wanting more than to touch, to feel, to give in to the hot, insistent ache that begged for fulfilment.

His lips drifted from her mouth, trailing down to the curve of her neck. He released her head, then gripped her hips to mould her body to his. "Don't ever threaten to leave me," he whispered in her ear.

"Don't ever dismiss me again," she threw back.

She felt his lips curve as he kissed beneath her ear. He lifted her off the floor and set her on the desk, her legs parted around him and her dress bunched around her hips. His fingers trailed up along her thighs, stopping only when they came to the juncture between her legs. She moaned when he touched her, and he kissed her again.

She could barely breathe. Caught between his fingers and his lips, she was nothing but a shuddering mass of pleasure. She gripped his powerful shoulders as her body rolled and jerked under his touch.

He released her lips and gazed down at her. "You're mine," he whispered.

"Yes," she moaned, helpless.

He kissed her again, and soon there was nothing...only his fingers, his touch, and the unending pleasure.

Her body started to shudder. "I'm yours," she cried out, losing herself to the pleasure. "Yours."

He nodded and withdrew his fingers, and just before she could start to beg for more, he drew her pliant body to the very edge of the table and drove himself deep inside her.

Her head fell back, only his arms keeping her from falling back on the hard surface of the desk.

"Hope." He said her name softly, his body shuddering as he started to move.

Her response was a long, shuddering moan of pure pleasure.

He sighed and buried his face in the curve of her neck, kissing her gently as he made love to her. Sensations spread like wildfire through her limbs and she held him tight, unwilling to let go, for any reason.

Pleasure rose again and again, exploding in a wild burst and starting all over again, until she was too weak, too weak to even moan his name.

He didn't stop until she had absolutely surrendered, to the pleasure, to her desire, to him... only then did he let himself go, losing control as he surrendered right along with her.

SHE DOZED OFF LATER, after Daniel carried her up

to his bed and made love to her again. There was something primal about their lovemaking. Like all the trappings of modernity had been wiped away, and it was just a man, claiming a woman as his.

Only his.

She woke up to silence. The low hum of the cool air coming in through the vents was the only sound. She went to the bathroom and dressed. She had no idea where Daniel was or what he was doing or thinking.

She wasn't even sure what *she* was thinking.

What had just happened?

Somewhere, there was probably a relationship manual that advised conversation instead of physical intimacy to resolve arguments, and the author was perfectly right.

"I'm yours," she whispered to her reflection in the mirror. And she was, however, he wanted her. The thought was both scary and exhilarating.

I won't share you with anyone else.

And he would never need to, because no one would ever come close.

Not Charles, not anybody else. No matter what happened.

She wondered where he was. They still needed to talk, so she went downstairs to find him. He wasn't in his study, or anywhere in the house. In the living room, her purse was on the sofa, along with her phone, where a blinking light showed that she had a new message.

From Daniel.

I've gone to the office. Samson is waiting outside to drive you home. Daniel.

There was no explanation, no assurance that he would see her later, or that they would talk about tonight. Hope read the text and swallowed the lump in her throat.

So that was it?

She'd hoped that they would talk, but instead he'd chosen to send her on her way like a booty call that had overstayed her welcome.

Her body was still flushed from the pleasure of his lovemaking, yet, she had never felt so abandoned.

CHAPTER NINETEEN

THAT NIGHT, she barely slept. The next day, she accompanied her parents to church and afterwards stayed in her room, only coming out to eat.

"What's doing you?" Grace asked her, later in the afternoon, when she drove over to pick up a beloved toy one of the children had left behind the day before. "Mummy said you're acting like a widow."

"Is there anything that woman doesn't see?" Hope sighed, rising from where she had burrowed into the covers on her bed. "I thought I was doing a good job of hiding myself in my room."

"Ha!" Grace laughed. "Someone that is already preparing for your wedding. If you derail her plans by not making this relationship work, she might dis-child you."

Hope laughed despite the pain. "Is that even a word?"

"Disown, then."

"She could," Hope said dourly. "I'll bet she could."

"Anyway," Grace gave her a concerned look. "What's the matter?"

"Where do I even start?" Hope said, doing her best to share most of what happened, only leaving out some of the more intimate parts.

"Your life is like a romance novel," Grace observed, amused.

"It's not funny."

"Okay." There was a pause. "He sounds very possessive."

Hope sighed. "To be fair, I feel very possessive about him too."

Grace's eyes probed her face. "I asked you some time ago if you were over Charles, and you said yes."

"I am over him."

"So why did you let him get to you? Why did you allow yourself to get so angry? Don't tell me it was because of Agnes."

"It was because of Agnes."

"No, it wasn't." Grace dismissed the excuse. "Agnes is not a child. She's seen what Charles is. She's had an encounter with his wife. She's not inexperienced. She doesn't need a saviour, and this is likely not her first ill-advised relationship."

"But she's my friend," Hope stared at her sister. "Was I supposed to just let her..."

"Make her own mistakes?" Grace nodded. "Yes. She doesn't need you to tell her what she already knows. You know that more than anyone, Hope. How many people tried to tell you about Charles? You never listened. Why do you think she will?"

Hope was quiet.

"If it was any other man, not Charles. Would you have been so bothered?"

"No, but..." She threw up her hands. "I was bothered because I know Charles is doing it to get to me. It was clear."

"Why are you so sure?" Grace said. "Agnes is attractive. He could want her for herself, and why do you care if Charles is trying to get to you? He shouldn't be able to...unless you're still holding on to what he did to you."

"I'm not..."

"Aren't you?"

Hope closed her eyes. She remembered the day of Ebisan's party. She'd wanted so much to put Charles in his place, to wipe the smile off his face, and when she'd seen him with Agnes, she'd felt cheated, like he had won a prize in a game where he should have ended up with nothing.

She'd ignored her own prize, temporarily forgotten about what she had, because she let her resentment cloud her vision.

"You should be indifferent to him, and it doesn't look like you are, and Daniel probably sees that." Grace shrugged. "If Charles can trigger you, he still has a hold on you."

Hope swallowed. She wanted to argue, but she knew when she was beaten.

"Nobody wants to be second choice, you know," Grace continued. "So, I understand his concern about Charles. It's weird for an ex to be so present in a relationship." She counted on her fingers. "He ran into you and Charles at a party. He took you to dinner when Charles stood you up. He saw Charles almost assault you at your friend's party, and now he sees you reacting so angrily to Charles dating your friend. It's almost like he's trying to date you and Charles."

Hope bristled. "It sounds like you think I'm to blame."

"Not everything has to have one person wrong, and one person right," Grace shrugged. "Put yourself in his shoes."

He made love to me. He told me I was his. He saw me at my most vulnerable, then he walked away.

Hope sniffed. "What about my own shoes?"

Grace rolled her eyes. "You just have to decide what's most important to you. Your pain and resentment from the past, or what Daniel promises for the future."

"I want the future with Daniel," she said softly. "A chance at least. More than anything, but what if he doesn't want it anymore?"

Grace chuckled. "Of course he does. Show him how much he matters to you, then go on from there."

AFTER THE CONVERSATION with her sister, Hope wrestled with her desire to call Daniel. He'd left her with no explanation and hadn't reached out to her. She had no way of knowing what he was thinking. If she reached out and his response was cold or brusque, she wasn't sure how she would bear it.

She knew the sweet parts of him, the part that brought her gifts and made her feel like a queen, but coming face to face with the cold, restrained anger, she was no longer sure how well she knew him. Had he made love to her knowing that it would break her when he walked away? Was he cold enough to punish her like that, deliberately? Was his current silence a dismissal?

The buzzing of her phone interrupted her thoughts. It was a message from Daniel.

Hi.

Her fingers shook as she typed a response.

Hi.

I won't be in the office tomorrow. Travelling for a meeting in the morning.

When will you be back? When will I see you? Why did you leave me alone last night? Are you aware that we need to resolve what happened? Do you even want to?

Her mind churned with questions. She wanted more than anything, to reach across the gulf that now separated them and feel his love again.

Okay, she typed. *I'll see you when you get back.*

There was a long pause where she could see the dots as he typed a long message. Then they disappeared.

Goodnight.

That was all.

THE NEXT DAY AT WORK, Agnes treated her to a

stony silence. Just before lunchtime, Hope went over to her desk.

"Can we talk?"

Agnes scowled. "No."

Hope sighed. She'd expected the resistance, so she soldiered on. "I know you're angry, and I'm sorry for what I said on Saturday. I shouldn't have implied that the only reason he wants to be with you is to make me jealous. You're a wonderful person, Agnes, and I admire and respect you. Any sensible man would too." Of course, Charles wasn't a sensible man, but it was neither the time nor place to mention that.

Agnes pursed her lips, but she seemed a little taken aback by the apology. "So, you're not angry that I'm still seeing him?"

You're not angry.

Angry.

She's been angry on Saturday night. Grace was right. Daniel had seen that. Charles had seen that. Agnes had too. She'd been angry, because she'd still been holding on to Charles and what he did to her.

Up till then, she hadn't wanted to forget him. She'd wanted to punish him.

And seeing him with Agnes had felt like he was getting away with everything. What he did to her, what he did to his wife, what he did to Agnes.

But they all chose to be with him, despite his lies...and now she could choose to leave him behind.

"People warned me about him, but I never listened. I always blamed him, but it was me who wanted to be blind. You're not a child." Hope smiled at Agnes. "Nobody can tell you what's best for you unless you decide to see it."

"Charles told me you're jealous because he dumped you years ago, and that you threw yourself at him when he met you again, and he didn't know how to let you down gently." Agnes said, watching Hope's face. "He said that when I called him, he knew he wanted to be with me, so he dumped you for me."

Hope chuckled. There was a deep sadness that Agnes believed the lies, but there was really nothing she could do about it.

"If you believe that," Hope said, "then I guess it's fine."

She went back to her desk, and they didn't talk again before Agnes left early for the day. Hope knew Agnes would come to her senses at some point and leave Charles behind, but by the time that happened, their friendship would probably never be the same.

THE DAY WENT ON, slowly, and she didn't hear from Daniel throughout. By evening, she missed him so much it felt like someone had sawed half of her body away with a rusty knife.

Her phone rang just as she was getting ready to leave the office.

"Hi, Hope." The voice on the phone was cheerful. "It's Ceecee."

"Hello," Hope replied, wondering why Daniel's friend was calling.

"Are you still at work?" Ceecee asked. "I got your number from Daniel's assistant. I hope you don't mind, but Daniel is out of reach."

"It's fine," Hope said. "It's great to hear from you."

"When do you finish from work?" Ceecee continued. "My sister is opening her restaurant on the Island this evening, and everyone will be there. I invited Daniel a long time ago and I'm sure you two would have come together, but since he's out of reach, I thought I should ask you."

"It's today?" Hope asked.

"Yes, I know it's sudden, but please say you'll come," she added in a pouty baby voice, making Hope laugh. "It'll be fun."

"Okay. I'll be there."

She arrived at the opening about an hour later,

meeting Ceecee and Temi at the door. The restaurant was in one of the quiet streets inside Victoria Island, perfect for the lunch crowd in need of something more sustaining than a snack. Music pumped from the speakers, while Temi rescued three bowls of Asun from a passing waiter, handing one each to Hope and Ceecee.

"Shey you'll tell your colleagues about this place," Ceecee said. "Epp my sister's business."

Hope laughed and glanced at Ceecee's sister, who was bustling around making sure the waiters served everybody. She was dripping in expensive jewellery, with skin as smooth as silk. She didn't look as if she needed any help for her business.

"I'll tell them," Hope assured Ceecee.

"You must miss Daniel terribly," Temi said. "I remember when Deinde and I first started dating, any absence was like torture. God knows...I felt like I could give up my whole life and follow him anywhere."

Ceecee's eyes widened. "Me too. There should be a cure for that feeling...a drug to prevent women from making stupid decisions at that sweet stage of love."

It wouldn't work, Hope thought, laughing along with them. Love was a crazy thing. One minute you were confident you knew exactly who you were, the next, everything had changed, and it felt like your whole world revolved around the object of your love.

"I miss him," Hope said, trying to smile over the ache deep inside her. *I miss him so much it hurts.*

"Awwww," Ceecee patted her hand. "Eat asun. You'll feel better."

Hope chuckled and took another mouthful. The flavours were wonderful, but no consolation for missing Daniel.

More people arrived. Hope and the girls found a corner of the party where they could gist with little disturbance while eating copious amounts of food.

They talked about work. Ceecee ran a thriving office supplies business and had inside gossip from some of the biggest firms on the island. Temi worked in financial services, was attending business school and had even juicier gossip.

Hope was laughing at something Ceecee said, when she had an uncanny feeling of eyes on her back. She turned around to see who it was and locked eyes with a woman who looked around her age or younger. She was beautifully dressed, obviously wealthy, and her eyes raked Hope with a venomous intensity.

Hope turned back from the familiar face. She'd never met her, but she knew that face because of all the hours she'd spent crying over Charles's wedding pictures on the internet.

It was his wife.

Ceecee was still talking, but Hope was barely listening. For a long time, she'd resented that face, blamed it for the loss of her *true love*.

Now, she only felt sad for the woman, and regretful of all the ill-feelings she'd directed towards her, when the real reason for her heartbreak had been no one but Charles...

...and herself, for closing her eyes to the truth.

She wished she could somehow communicate all that to Charles' wife, but of course that was impossible. The woman obviously knew who she was, and judging from that venomous stare, still blamed Hope, and possibly every other woman, for her husband's infidelities.

"What are you thinking about?" Temi sounded concerned.

Hope grimaced slightly. "Nothing, just work."

She sneaked a glance behind her again, but Charles wife was no longer standing there. Shrugging the incident out of her mind, she spent the rest of the evening trying to enjoy herself instead of focusing on the distance between herself and Daniel.

Temi got up to leave first. Deinde had come to

pick her up and expressed regret that he hadn't been able to attend the party.

"Thanks for coming," Ceecee smiled at Hope as Deinde drove off.

Hope shrugged. "I enjoyed myself, and the food was spectacular."

"Right?" Ceecee hugged the small bump of her belly and laughed. "Right on time too. I need all the free meals I can get." She peered at Hope. "Is everything all right with you and Daniel? You looked a bit sober when we teased you about him earlier."

Was it so obvious?

"You know," Ceecee continued, "Daniel can be a rigid, workaholic, bore sometimes, but he's crazy about you. You know that right?"

Hope smiled sadly. "I'm crazy about him too."

"Obviously," Ceecee laughed. "I've known Daniel since Uni, and he's always been focused on some big goal. First, graduation, then work, saving for masters, travelling out, setting up his company. I've seen him achieve big things, but I haven't ever seen him as happy and relaxed as when he's with you."

There was a small flutter of pleasure inside her, but Hope stayed silent.

"This sounds like those speeches guys give their friend's babes, right?" Ceecee smiled. "It's not though. He's crazy about you. It's true. Pregnant women never lie."

Hope laughed. "I'll take your word for it."

"You'll see," Ceecee said. They walked over to Hope's car. "I'm going back inside to eat some more. Drive safe...and say hi to Daniel when you see him."

They hugged and Hope watched Ceecee walk back inside the brightly lit interior of the restaurant. She started her car, wondering if Daniel had returned. Coming face to face with Charles's wife and the reality of his duplicity, contrasted with the image of Daniel, resolute, driven and now, entirely focused on her, she could see clearly how different Daniel was. How special.

She was already calling him when her phone rang. She accepted the call, her heart aching just at the sight of his name on her screen.

"Hope." He said her name only. She'd missed the sound of his voice so much, hearing it made her heart twist.

"Hey," she said through stinging eyes.

"How are you?"

"Good." She paused. "I've been at a party with Ceecee and Temi. It wasn't bad. The food was great...and the girls were fun." She was rambling but she couldn't stop herself.

"Oh...the restaurant," he said. "I told her I'd come."

"She knows you travelled."

"Yeah." There was a short silence. "I am back."

"Oh..." She wondered where he was. At home, or at the office. She wanted to see him, so badly.

"Are you still at the party?" he asked.

"Just leaving."

"I'm at the office," he said. "I can come there and get you."

"No. I'll come to you."

She heard him inhale. "I'll be waiting."

It only took a few minutes to reach the office. She parked close to the entrance and walked into the lobby, a heavy tenseness making her belly feel frozen. The place was almost deserted, with only some of the security staff, some people on their way out, and Daniel.

He was standing at the other end of the lobby from the entrance, and as she walked inside, their eyes met.

I love him.

The realisation flowed through her like a torrent. Maybe it had taken the distance of the past few days to make her see just how important he was to her. She knew that she wouldn't...couldn't ever walk away from him.

He came toward her, his long legs eating up the distance in mere seconds. There was something about him...his air of purpose and yet more, that made other people stop and stare. Hope waited, her heart pounding wildly, anticipation making her weak.

When he reached her, he pulled her gently into his arms, and without saying a word, covered her lips with his.

CHAPTER TWENTY

"I'm sorry," he said later, upstairs in his office.

Hope touched a finger to her tingling lips. "Why," she gave him a small teasing smile. "For kissing me in front of people who will no doubt be talking about it tomorrow?"

He waved a dismissive hand. "Of course not. I don't care if the whole world talks about it. I mean, last weekend, at my place." His eyes met hers. "For the whole thing, for leaving too."

"I'm sorry too," Hope said. "You were right about my reaction to seeing Charles with Agnes. It was unnecessary. I understand why you reacted the way you did."

"You're too forgiving," he smiled gently and came toward her. "I was being self-righteous and judgemental, full of my expectations and lacking any understanding."

Hope laughed. "When you put it like that, how can I not let you take all the blame."

He touched his forehead to hers. "I missed you."

"I missed you too." She sighed. She had to tell him she'd left Charles behind. "Daniel..."

He put a hand on her lips. "Don't. Not now." He took her in his arms. "I don't want explanations. I just want to be with you."

He kissed her, and she let all the words fall away. For the moment, at least, it was just enough to be with him.

"Hope!" Mrs Amadi's face lit up in a bright smile. "You look even prettier than the last time I saw you." She drew Hope into her arms for a hug, then turned to Daniel who was a few steps behind Hope. "You finally brought her to see us, abi?"

Daniel laughed and hugged his mother. "I didn't know it was a matter of urgency."

"I didn't know it was a matter of urgency," His mother repeated, mimicking his voice. "I don't know who this boy is speaking English for."

Hope giggled. Just then, Daniel's father walked

into the room. He was a tall man, with a full head of shiny silvery grey hair. Daniel looked almost exactly like him.

"Good evening," Hope said.

"Good evening, Dad."

"Good evening." He looked from Daniel to Hope. "So you're Hope," he said. "Come. Come." He gave her a light hug. "My wife has been looking forward to your visit. Welcome."

"Thank you."

He turned a glance at Daniel. "Congratulations," he said.

Hope turned to look at Daniel, who was smiling but silent. What was *he* being congratulated about?

Just then, Daniel's younger brother Phillip burst into the room with the energy of youth. At least ten years younger than Daniel, he was literally the baby of the house.

After all the introductions were over, they went to the dining room to have lunch.

"Daniel said you're an engineer," his father asked Hope.

"Yes, Mechanical."

He nodded. "That's impressive."

"When I was in school, there were about two girls in the whole of mechanical engineering. Accounting, my course, had a reputation for being tough, but it was nothing like engineering," his wife added.

Hope nodded in agreement. "In my set, there were just six of us in a class of a hundred and twenty, or so. Things haven't changed that much. There are more girls in electrical and computer engineering though. Mechanical just has a reputation for being hard."

"And it's not?" Mr Amadi asked.

"Oh, it is, hard, but not impossible."

"So you guys work in the same building," Phillip said. "That must be very convenient."

Daniel narrowed his eyes at his younger brother, but there was a slight smile on his lips. "Convenient for what?"

Phillip's eyes widened innocently. "I don't know...seeing each other?"

Daniel chuckled. "Yeah, right."

"Whatever you think I was going to say..." Phillip said mischievously. "It says more about you than about me."

"Children of nowadays," Daniel sounded amused. "No respect."

After lunch, they went back to the living room. Phillip went out, and Daniel and his father disappeared for a little while, probably to talk.

Mrs Amadi retrieved some old photo albums from a shelve and brought them to show Hope.

She guffawed at the baby picture of Daniel. "Look how cute he is." She turned the page, and there was another picture of baby Daniel with his mother, only the woman in the picture didn't look very much like Mrs Amadi.

"Is that you?" Hope asked before she could stop herself.

Daniel's mother gave her a curious look. "That's his mother. Biological mother to him and Stephanie." She frowned. "He hasn't mentioned her to you?"

Hope shook her head. "I didn't know."

Mrs Amadi sighed. "I'm sure he plans to tell you at some point. It's not something he likes to talk about."

Hope gazed at the woman in the photo album. She was beautiful, with Daniel's wide dark eyes and dark skin that glowed with health. "Did something happen to her?"

There was a pause, as if the older woman wasn't quite sure whether to tell her. "She left when he was six...and she died when he was a teenager."

"She left?" Hope couldn't wrap her mind around a mother leaving Daniel. "I didn't know."

"He'll tell you in his own time, dear. Okay?"

Hope nodded, and they looked at the rest of the

pictures until Daniel returned to the living room with his father.

"Come and visit us any time you want," Mrs Amadi told Hope later, when they were leaving. "And I would love to meet your parents too." There were a few more hugs, and then she and Daniel were in his car, driving back to his place.

"I can't believe I was nervous before," Hope told Daniel. "Your parents are awesome."

"I am awesome," he said. "I had to get it from somewhere, didn't I?"

Hope smiled.

"That looks like a sad smile," Daniel said. "What's going on?"

"Nothing," Hope said. He gave her a look that said he wasn't fooled, so she continued. "Your mom told me a little about your biological mother. I was looking at some of your baby pictures and saw her."

Daniel was quiet.

"Why didn't you tell me?"

"Because I have only one mother, and you just met her."

There was an unmistakable harshness in his voice. "I'm sorry," Hope said.

"Why?"

"Because she died."

Daniel shrugged. "She left." There was a pause.

"I don't want to talk about it."

"Okay." Hope could feel the tension emanating from him. It was obviously a sore topic.

"I hope you don't blame your mom for telling me."

"It's not a big deal." He stopped at an intersection and turned to look at her. "Let's not spoil today by dwelling on it."

She had more questions, but she allowed him to change the subject. At his place, Hope followed him upstairs to his bedroom. She took off her shoes and curled up on one side of the bed, switching on the TV while he changed out of his clothes into a t-shirt and sweatpants.

She flicked through channels, and when he came to lie beside her on the bed, she turned to face him. "I'm glad we went to see your parents," she said. "I feel like I know you a bit more."

He snickered. "You already know me very well."

"You mean biblically?"

He grinned. "Isn't that the best kind of knowing?"

"I'm not sure..." she started, then shrieked in surprise when he pulled her into his arms.

"I'm going to give you a demonstration," he said. "So you can decide."

Hope giggled, remote forgotten. "I like demonstrations."

Daniel kissed her long and deep. When he lifted his head, there was a tenderness in his eyes that made her heart ache. "I love you," he murmured.

His voice was deep and soft, but the words burned through her like a flame. Tears filled her eyes, and she drew in a breath.

"I love you too."

He kissed her again. "Now that we've established all that," he said with a devilish grin, "Time for some biblical knowing."

Hope tittered. "Oh, if you insist."

He laughed. "I do."

CHAPTER TWENTY-ONE

"You guys are making me really really aware of the fact that I'm single," Briggs complained, glaring at Hope and Daniel. They were at a party for his uncle's sixtieth birthday, and all around, everything was bubbling owambe style, with a never-ending flow of music, food and drinks.

Daniel had been whispering in Hope's ear, making her giggle. Now, he faced Briggs. "It's not my fault you're single. Why don't you do something about it and stop disturbing me and my girlfriend?"

"Nah," Briggs shook his head. "I'm too young and beautiful to settle down."

Everyone at the table burst into laughter.

"Someone has been deceiving you," Ceecee said. "Young and beautiful where?"

Briggs looked hurt. "I'm going to find a really

pretty girl to dance with." He got up and stroked his face. "Someone who appreciates a guy with a connected beard."

That resulted in another round of teasing. Briggs walked away, laughing.

"Are you enjoying yourself?" Daniel asked Hope.

"Yes." She gave him a contented smile. The music was lively, and food and drinks were flowing. Brigg's uncle's home was just off the Lekki expressway, and the large garden now housed a large air-conditioned tent where the party was taking place. "I love the live band."

Daniel didn't reply, but his eyes stayed on her face. She met his gaze, a half smile playing on her lips as memories of shared intimacy floated lazily across her brain.

"I want to kiss you," he whispered.

Hope chuckled. "Sure, give your friends something to tease you about."

"They tease me enough already," he chuckled and speared a piece of suya with a skewer, then held it up to her lips. "Have you tasted this?"

She took a bite. "Delicious," she said, licking her lips slowly.

He sighed. "You're killing me."

"Are you sure you guys won't go and get a room?" Uche said, lips pursed.

"They're acting romantic movie for us," Temi added. "Get a room. Ceecee's baby will need a little someone to play with."

"Shey you, you're forbidding to do your own and give my baby a playmate," Ceecee said to Temi. "Hope, abeg leave that man for a few minutes, let's go and look for the bathroom."

Hope stood, laughing as Daniel held on to her waist, refusing to let her go.

"I go love oooo!" Ceecee said, laughing.

Uche gestured toward her stomach. "Which love is more than this belle I've already given you?"

Hope was still laughing as she, Ceecee and Temi navigated the party, finding their way into the main house to the guest bathroom on the ground floor.

"You guys look so happy," Temi said to Hope. "So good together."

Hope smiled. "Thanks. It feels good too."

"Sha hurry up and give my baby a playmate." Ceecee said. "Temi is not ready."

Hope laughed. "When the time comes, don't worry."

"Can you hear?" Temi told Ceecee. "When the time comes."

Later, they headed back to the tent, still talking.

They were right on the edge of the white structure when Hope heard a familiar voice.

"Hope."

She stiffened. If she had been alone, she would have ignored him and kept walking, but Temi and Ceecee had already stopped and turned toward the voice.

Charles was standing at the edge of the tent, near the hedge of flowers that lined the fence. He had his phone in his hand like he had been making a call, and he was looking at Hope with a benign expression of pleasant surprise.

"Hi," Hope replied. She kept her voice light and pleasant for the sake of her companions. Ceecee and Temi waved politely as Charles walked toward them.

"You know him?" Temi asked. There was a hint of protectiveness in her voice.

Hope nodded. What else could she say? If she kept walking now, it would only arouse their curiosity, and she wasn't ready to answer questions about Charles. It was far more prudent to just exchange a few polite words with him and go back inside.

"Okay," Ceecee said. "Let's leave you guys to say hi. We'll see you back at the table, okay?"

Temi hesitated, looking at Hope's face as if waiting for a sign to make her stay, but Ceecee took her hand and they headed inside the huge party tent.

Charles looked pleased. "How're you doing?"

Hope shrugged. Outside the tent there were a few other stragglers from the party; servers and a few teenagers showing each other stuff on their phones.

"I'm fine," she said evenly. Her mind went to Agnes, who was still not talking to her. She'd seen her crying at her desk a few times, but she stayed away from the matter of Charles. Whenever Agnes wanted to talk about it, she'd be there.

He stood looking at her, and she met his gaze in silence. The beauty that had enslaved her for so long now seemed empty and weak, overshadowed by the lies he told and the games he played.

"Do you have something to say, or..." She raised questioning eyebrows. "People are waiting for me inside."

"Like who? Your rich boyfriend?" There was a sneer in his voice.

Hope didn't reply.

"Hope. Come on..." he cajoled. "I just want to talk to you."

"I'm still waiting for you to say anything worth listening to."

"Let's go somewhere..."

"Private?" Hope gave him a pitying smile. "Your game has really not changed, has it? Get me somewhere private, lie, seduce, then feel powerful afterwards. That's what you really need isn't it, to feel like you have power over women, because deep down you know you're powerless, ineffective, inferior...weak?"

He looked taken aback. "Watch your mouth. We both know I'd only need to touch you and your words wouldn't be so sharp anymore. You'd be begging me to continue."

Once maybe. Now the thought of his touch made her skin crawl.

"Go away, Charles. Grow up. At some point your life has to stop being about how many women you can get to want you." She smiled. "Bye."

"Don't go," he blurted. There was a new and sudden edge of desperation in his voice. "Look, I know you hate me, but you don't know how it is. You have no idea."

Hope stepped back, but he only moved closer. "Charles–"

"Do you know what it's like to feel trapped? With someone who sees you as a possession, an accessory. She doesn't care about my feelings. She doesn't care about what I think. As long as she has a *husband*. That's all I am Hope, a word to make her feel like she has fulfilled some expectations of her as a woman."

An image of his wife's angry face entered her thoughts. He was lying, obviously. A woman who didn't care wouldn't stakeout hotel rooms and glare at ex-girlfriends. His wife's supposed disinterest had always been just one of his ploys.

"I don't know what you want me to say," she said. She had no intention of being a crutch to help him through his misery, real or fake. "You made your choices, Charles. The best you can do is learn to live with them."

His laugh was bitter. "So, I have to be miserable for the rest of my life?" His voice softened. "You've become heartless, Hope. What happened to all the love, all the feelings you had for me?"

He had never looked as unattractive to her as he did right at that moment. He was a liar and a cheat. A manipulator. He would never take responsibility for his own happiness, but he would blame and cajole other people to give him the things he needed to make himself feel good. Their time, their bodies, their feelings... How had she not seen it all those years? How had she never realised what he was?

Disgust filled her insides, and without a word, she turned and started to walk away.

He grabbed her arm and pulled her to him, holding her tight against his body.

"I still want you," he said in a low voice. "I always will. Can't you feel it?"

She could feel the evidence of his arousal pressed against her hip. Bile rose in her throat and she kicked him hard on the shin. She wrenched herself free, moments before she heard the female voice from the edge of the tent, high and disbelieving. "Charles!"

He froze, and Hope turned toward the newcomer, his wife, whose face was crumpling as she stared at Charles. Then, she turned to Hope, and her expression went from hurt and betrayal to visceral hatred.

"You!" she said, her voice high. "You! Why won't you leave my husband alone. Why are you so desperate? Leave him alone!" her voice broke on a sob.

Hope stared at her, momentarily short of words.

"You're a slut! You're shameless! He's told me about you. He dumped you for a reason. Leave him alone! Don't you have any shame? Why can't you stop chasing him? He's married now. We have a newborn baby!"

She should have been angry at the woman for

speaking to her like that. She should have felt affronted, but all Hope felt was pity.

This would have been me, she thought. This *would* have been me, married to Charles and blaming other women because accepting the reality that the love of my life was a cheating, lying, weakling would have been too much for me to bear.

She held on to that compassion as the woman continued to insult her. They were a few people outside the tent, and more were gathering even though the noise of the live band drowned out most of the shouting.

"Don't you have anything to say for yourself?" the woman said. "You were embracing him. Right here. A married man. Do you know what that makes you?" her face contorted. "It makes you a prostitute."

"You are wrong," Hope said calmly.

Instead of calming Charles' wife, Hope's words seemed to inflame her, and she lunged at her. Charles, unsurprisingly did nothing to stop her. It was Daniel, arriving just at that moment, who stepped in front of Hope. Charles' wife lost her balance, falling toward him, and as he held out his arms and steadied her, she started to cry.

"Get your hands off my wife," Charles blustered angrily.

Daniel stepped back from the weeping woman.

He glared at Charles, who wilted under the force of his gaze. "Don't ever let me see you near Hope again," Daniel warned, his voice low.

Charles sneered. "She was mine before she ever met you. We've shared things that—"

"You've shared what?" Daniel interrupted. "Man, have some shame and stop disgracing yourself and your wife."

Charles seemed to deflate. Hurriedly, he took his wife's arm, but she jerked it back and started walking away. He followed her.

She would forgive him, Hope thought sadly. He would lie and she would forgive, again and again and again, until one day it would all be too much and she would break. Poor woman.

Daniel was scanning the small crowd that had gathered. Some of them were making videos, Hope noticed. Hope sighed inwardly. She didn't need a fortune teller to divine that he was probably very pissed off.

"Daniel—"

"Let's go." His voice was curt, and she could feel the anger radiating from his body. She could see it in the tense set of his shoulders, the hard line of his jaw...she could feel it in the silence as he walked ahead to where he parked his car.

She followed him, also silent.

They reached the car, and he started to open the door. Hope stood at the passenger side.

"Daniel..." She started. "I don't know what it looked like to you, but if you'd just let me explain what happened..."

He stopped and glared at her over the roof of the car. "Go on. Explain how I just prevented you from getting into a catfight over your ex."

Hope sighed. "That...Don't make this into something it's not."

"I shouldn't..." He made a frustrated sound. "How many times are we going to be in this same situation, Hope?"

"I didn't create the situation," Hope countered. "It's not like I invited him to Brigg's uncle's party."

"No," he said wryly. "But somehow, you two found each other. You always do."

"Don't do this."

"Do what? React to the effects of your bad decisions?"

"My bad decisions?"

"Yes, Hope. Your bad decisions. You chose to open the door for this loser to come back into your life. You chose to ignore everything that had happened between you two before. That's all you, and if you're going to keep making excuses and finding reasons to let him into your life, then..." He caught himself and stopped.

"Then what?"

He took a deep breath. "Hope, I don't want to fight. Can we just leave?"

She stared at him, tears filling her eyes. Yes, she'd opened the door for Charles to come back into her life. Yes, she'd held on to her anger and betrayal and jumped at the opportunity to make him beg, to revel in him wanting her again, she'd let him in, even though she'd known he was married, even though she'd known deep down that he hadn't changed.

But she'd gone past all that. She'd let go of the anger and hurt and she had let Charles go. The only person who wasn't seeing that was Daniel.

She got into the car. A moment later, he joined her.

"Please take me home," she mumbled.

"Hope..."

She shook her head. "Don't. I don't feel like talking anymore."

He drove in silence to the mainland. At her house, he parked on the street and the silence stretched.

"You're right I made a lot of bad decisions, especially when I let Charles back into my life. I've accepted that. I was angry. I wanted to punish him for leaving me. I wanted to make him want me desperately again...and I was wrong for that, but I never expected you to throw it in my face like you did back there."

"Hope..."

"I have let him go, Daniel. I let go of the anger, of the need to make him pay. I realised how unimportant he was to me." She swallowed. "I meant every word when I said that I was yours, but I can't live every day trying to keep proving that I belong to you. I'm not going to cage myself and walk around on eggshells trying to prove that I'm yours. If you don't trust me, if any unimportant shadow from my past can come between us..." She sighed. "I'm not going to keep turning myself inside out to prove things to you you shouldn't even doubt."

His chest rose. "I'm not asking you to live like that."

"You were going to give me an ultimatum back there!" Her voice rose. "What were you going to say? That if I'm going to keep letting him into my life... you don't want to be a part of it?"

He looked at her. "If you're going to keep letting him into your life...then no, I don't. I told you, that I'd never share you."

"You'd rather just let me go." She swallowed. "And what constitutes letting him back into my life,

Daniel? A conversation I didn't invite? An altercation his wife started? Am I going to keep atoning for the *bad decisions* in my past by always being at fault for whatever he does?"

Daniel was silent.

"If you trusted me, you wouldn't find it so hard to believe when I tell you I love you, that I am yours, that I belong to you. His appearance or existence wouldn't be able to shake what we have."

He turned to face her. "Hope, I love you. A part of me loved you even from the first time I saw you, when I didn't even know who you were." He paused. "But I can't ignore the existence of another man who seems to have a hold on you."

"And I've told you he means nothing to me."

He didn't reply.

"Of course you don't believe me," Hope said bitterly. "You can't allow yourself to trust me, so you'd rather walk away. I have too much messy emotional baggage for you and your perfection."

"Don't be ridiculous..."

"I'm just saying it as I see it. You're so perfect, so I have to be perfect too. No scenes. No Exes. No issues from the past. Well, guess what, you're not perfect either. Have you asked yourself why you care so much about an ex who means nothing to me anymore? Why you can't bear to talk about your biological mother? Why you're so freaking self-righteous? I'm flawed, Daniel, and so are you."

His jaw hardened, and she wondered if she'd gone too far, but she continued. "I'm flawed. And if you built me up as a paragon in your head before you could love me, I am not one. I'm not a paper ideal that you could put on a pedestal. I'm not some ready-made-for-commitment type of girl who ticks all the boxes for a successful guy wanting to settle down. I'm not the goody-goody-never-been-touched *wife material* who'll complement your perfect life and cause no problems for you."

For a long while, he said nothing. The silence stretched, and she waited for something, anything to change the direction the day was going.

It started to rain, suddenly. One minute, everything was quiet, and the next, huge drops of water started to hit the glass outside the car.

Daniel put the car in drive, then hit the horn. Ayuba opened the gate and still not saying a word, he drove inside the compound, parking under the canopy of the carport as the rain sounded all around them like a dirge for their failing relationship.

"I know I'm not perfect, and I never asked you to be." he paused. "But if you think I only want you because you tick some imaginary boxes for someone I want to *settle down* with...if you think I only love the image of you I've built in my head...then why are you with me?"

Because I love you, the words stuck in her throat. *Because being with you means more to me than anything else. I love you so much I'd take you with every single flaw, and it wouldn't move my love one inch. I want you to see all my flaws and still love me, with no doubts and no reservations.*

"You should go inside." His voice was stiff.

Hope nodded. Her throat felt raw, and she wanted to cry.

Shakily, she opened the door and slid out of the car, and only when she was inside, in the solitude of her bedroom, did she finally allow the dam of tears to burst.

CHAPTER TWENTY-TWO

SHE SPENT most of the night crying, drifting into sleep a few times, only to wake up from painful dreams where Daniel walked away from her again and again, leaving her empty and broken. The next morning, with her eyes swollen from crying, Hope considered calling in sick and spending the whole day in bed. Only the thought of her mother's questions and concern pushed her out of the house.

Trying to keep her face from betraying her feelings was the hardest thing she'd ever done. Her insides felt bruised and shattered. She couldn't stop thinking about Daniel and every word they'd said to each other.

...Then why are you with me.

You should go inside.

The more she thought about the words, the more they felt like the end of their relationship.

Everything hurt. Her chest. The thought of him in the same building. The idea that maybe she'd gone too far. The distance...

She wanted to see him, to talk, but she knew they'd probably only argue again.

She was angry and hurt. She felt rejected, but the thought of losing him was a different kind of agony all together.

She wondered where he was.

Was he thinking about her?

Was he as destroyed as she was?

What if he didn't care?

What if, as far as he was concerned, they were already over?

Then maybe he never deserved you.

The thought offered no comfort.

She barely contributed in the morning meeting. Her mind and emotions kept churning. During all those years with Charles, she'd thought she knew what it meant for love to hurt. But she'd never felt like this, as if the world was an endless pit, and she was falling, unsure if the sickening descent would ever end.

Back at her desk, she stared at her screen, unable to focus on the lines and letters. She started to compose an email to Daniel. After a few sentences, she abandoned it. What would she say? What were the right words to say *I love you but I'm mad at you but I can't live without you.*

Again, she wondered where he was. The silence from him was driving her crazy. She needed to talk to him. She reached for her phone, then put it back down. She was a mess.

She got up and walked the length of the office, from one wall to another, from her desk to the water dispenser by the large windows. She stood there, her gaze fixed beyond the shutters at the streets of Victoria island below, then she walked back to her desk.

Focus. Focus.

She wished she could focus on anything else, wait out his silence until they were both ready to talk, really talk, not fight.

But she couldn't.

Every second of not knowing what was going on with them was like torture. She had to know what he was thinking.

She picked up her phone again and started to type a message. There was so much she wanted to say, about how he needed to trust her, how much he'd hurt her, how much she missed him...

She pressed send and stared at the message she'd typed.

Are we giving each other the silent treatment now? Is that how we're dealing with this?"

Her eyes watered. The message wasn't even close to what she wanted to say, but her feelings had gotten in the way. So now, he would think she was angry and lashing out.

She waited for him to respond, and as the seconds ticked by, a deep sadness set in.

She'd sounded like such a shrew.

That hadn't been her intention.

What if he didn't respond?

What would she do?

Relax Hope. He's only a man. He's not the last man on earth.

Stop fooling yourself. You know he's the only man for you.

The voices in her head were tortuous. She got up and walked toward the water dispenser again.

"Your pacing is giving me whiplash," one of her colleagues, Jide, said when she walked past his desk again. "Is everything all right?"

"Yes," Hope snapped.

He raised his eyebrows and went back to his computer. Agnes glanced at Hope. They had talked little since the day Hope apologised, and Hope had no idea what was going on in her life. So she was surprised when Agnes rose and walked over to meet her at the windows.

"Hey."

Hope folded her arms. "Hi."

"Is everything all right?"

Hope snorted. "We haven't spoken for weeks Agnes, now is not the time to rekindle our friendship."

Agnes sighed. "Fine. I'm sorry for everything, and for not listening to you about...him, and for believing all the other stuff. I just wanted to say that...and to tell you that you were right."

"Congratulations," Hope said wryly. "Early realisation means minimum destruction. Lucky you."

"Don't be mean," Agnes said. "It's very unlike you."

Hope felt her eyes sting. "I'm sorry... I'm just in a bad place right now. I'm glad you're out of whatever situation you were in with Charles."

"Yeah." Agnes shrugged. "Don't worry. Whatever it is...everything will be fine. You're a good person, Hope, and you're a good friend."

The hug that followed surprised Hope, and she watched Agnes walk back to her seat. Jide stopped her and said something to her, and they both laughed.

Well, at least one good thing might still come out of this whole situation, Hope thought.

Just then her phone beeped, and she unlocked it, hastily reading the message that had just come in.

It was from Daniel.

"We'll talk later."

Hope stared at the screen. Three words. Three words? After everything? She wanted to cry, to scream, something...anything to let out the mixture of pain, longing, panic, hurt, and loneliness she was feeling.

Three words. Did he not understand how she was feeling right now. Didn't he care? Didn't he feel the same way?

She went back to her desk and tried again to focus on a design project, but the lines blurred into one another as she fought back tears of frustration.

Her hand was shaking as she tried to move the mouse. She grabbed her phone and stared at his message again, then without thinking, typed a reply.

"What's the point?"

She waited for him to reply but seconds turned to minutes, then to an hour, then two, and she heard nothing from him.

She was so focused on her phone she didn't see Ladi approach her desk until the other woman was right in front of her.

Her heart surged. Maybe Daniel was out in the reception and wanted to see her.

"Security wants your car keys," Ladi said. "It's like you parked on top of one of the underground pipes and they want to work on it."

Disappointed, Hope gave the receptionist her keys and turned back to her screen.

"Your face is looking one-kind. Shey you're all right sha. All you single ladies your problem no dey ever dey pass man."

Hope glared, about to reply with a cutting remark, but the expression on Ladi's face stopped her. Her eyes were on something or someone behind Hope and she looked dumbfounded.

Somehow, Hope knew. Her stomach knotted, a sweet tension seizing hold of all her limbs. She wanted to turn her chair around, to stand up and see him, because she could already feel that he was here, coming toward her.

His shadow fell across her desk, but she still didn't swivel her chair.

"Good afternoon," Ladi croaked.

"Good afternoon," Daniel's voice was deep, polite, and without inflection, but it tugged at everything inside Hope. Slowly, she turned her chair around.

At the sight of him, her body filled with longing

and her eyes stung with unshed tears. There was no way she could live without this man. The very thought was like a knife in her chest.

He was dressed casually. Black jeans that hugged his slim hips and strong thighs, paired with a grey shirt that was fitted just enough to show off his athletic build. He didn't look like he'd been at work, and a part of her wondered why, while the other part ached to throw herself in his arms.

He met her gaze, and she felt something tearing at her heart. "Hope," he said simply.

She looked around the office and saw people hurriedly glancing back at their monitors. Ladi was still standing there, staring with a mixture of envy and avid interest.

"Uhm...Please come with me," Hope whispered shakily, before leading him toward one of the conference rooms.

Once they were inside, she shut the door and turned to face him. He looked worried, like he wasn't sure how she would receive whatever he planned to say. She wanted to walk into his arms and stay there, to forget that the weekend had happened at all.

"I got your text," he said quietly.

Hope sighed. "Daniel I was—"

He stopped her. "I'm sorry about the way I acted. I was hasty. I was quick to blame you for a situation that wasn't your fault. You have every right to be angry with me." He paused and closed his eyes. "You're right, I'm not perfect and I'm sorry I made you feel you had to be."

She let out a shaky breath. "Daniel, I..."

"What you said about my mother..."

"I'm sorry. I shouldn't have..."

"No." he shook his head. "You were right to mention it. I don't talk about her because I've never allowed myself to forgive her. I've been holding on to a lot of anger, and I let it cloud our relationship." He swallowed. "Before she left, she told my Dad that Stephanie wasn't his. She took Stephanie, but left me, and went back to her ex-boyfriend, who was Stephanie's biological father."

"Her ex," Hope repeated, understanding flooding her mind. Somewhere inside him was a little boy whose mother had walked away. A growing boy who'd lost his first symbol of feminine affection to an old lover.

An old lover.

Like Charles.

"He didn't want me," Daniel continued, "So she left me behind."

"I'm so sorry," Hope said.

"No, I am," he smiled sadly. "You made me realise that I was holding you responsible for the things I hadn't forgiven her for. I was refusing to trust you, because of what she did."

Hope sighed. They'd both allowed issues from the past to poison their present and almost destroy their future together.

"I should have told you." He continued. "Instead, I let myself stew in the idea that I was competing with your first love..."

"No," Hope shook her head. "Daniel, you *are* my first love."

His chest rose. "Hope," he said softly. He stepped forward, as if to take her in his arms, then he stopped. "Do you really think I built up a perfect image of you in my head? That I don't love you for who you are? That I only want you because I want to settle down?"

"No." Hope sighed. "Yes... I don't know. I've thought about it."

"Hope." He took her hand. "You don't fit any stereotype. You're special. You're different. I've never seen you as one of many possibilities, Hope. You've always been the one. I wasn't thinking of settling down when I first saw you, but when I did, I lost the ability to think. For months, I tried not to approach you because I wasn't sure I was ready for the way you made me feel. You make me want to forget everything, to know you as deeply as it is possible to know another person."

"Daniel..." Hope sniffed. There were tears in her eyes.

"I love everything about you," he said. "I love that you're beautiful and smart. You're curious, stubborn, loyal. I love how you talk about your family, how much you love them. I love that you complain about living with your parents, but secretly you love the way your mum hovers over you..." he smiled. "I love your lips, I love that your second toe is longer than your first. I love your tiny little snores."

Hope chuckled through her tears. "I don't snore."

Daniel laughed, then sobered again. "I didn't *pick you* because I was thinking of settling down, Hope, but I'm thinking about it now, because I don't want to contemplate my life without you."

Hope walked into his arms and buried her face in his chest. "I love you," she whispered. "I'm sorry and I love you."

He stroked her hair. "My interest is in you. I don't care about anything that happened before me."

Hope met his gaze. "Nobody matters to me but you."

He nodded slowly. "I love you." His voice was gentle.

"I love you," Hope replied, tightening her arms around him.

He sighed. "I hate to leave, but your colleagues will soon start wondering what we're doing in here."

Hope giggled. "Let them wonder." She paused. "How come you're dressed so casually?"

"I decided to work from home today."

She frowned. "Really?"

He nodded. "Yes. My girlfriend left my heart a bit tender over the weekend, so I stayed home to lick my wounds...until she compelled me, via a very alarming message, to come over and plead with her not to leave me."

"I'd never leave you," Hope laughed.

He kissed her again. "That's the best thing I've heard all day."

Luckily, she'd chosen the least used of all the conference rooms, so nobody had walked in on their conversation. They kissed goodbye and emerged together, ignoring the covert looks from people in the outer office.

"I'll see you later," Daniel said with a smile, then walked toward the entrance.

"Isn't that Daniel Amadi?"

Hope jumped, then turned to the voice. It was one of the senior partners and he was standing right beside her. She hadn't even seen him come out from his office.

"Yes...That's him."

The man peered into the empty conference room, then at Hope. "I wasn't aware we were doing any work for him."

"I...yes," Hope lied. "That's what we were meeting about. He wanted to discuss design possibilities for a site he's interested in. It's prone to flooding, and he wanted to get a feel of what was possible before engaging us formally."

The man nodded. "Good job then. I hope that means we'll be seeing more of him."

Hope smiled. "I hope so too."

CHAPTER TWENTY-THREE

THE REST of the day passed in a haze of happiness. Hope barely got any work done.

I love you.

I don't want to contemplate life without you.

You make me want to forget everything but you.

It was so gratifying to be in love with someone who loved her back with the same intensity.

"Apparently, whatever Daniel Amadi said to you changed your entire mood. You've gone from grumpy to blissful."

Agnes had shifted her chair as close to her desk as possible and looked like she wanted to be in on the gist.

Hope chuckled. "Is it so obvious?"

"Yes. You've been laughing and smiling to yourself since. Whatever you guys said...or did in that conference room..." Agnes wiggled her eyebrows suggestively. "It worked."

Hope laughed. "God knows I've missed you."

A ghost of sadness flitted over Agnes's face. "I missed you too."

Hope took her hand. "You know I'm always here if you want to talk."

Agnes shrugged. "Maybe, but not today. Today, I don't want to spoil your happy mood."

Later, after work, Hope drove over to Daniel's place. She'd only barely convinced him not to come back to the office to pick her up, and mere moments after she drove into his compound, he opened the front door. He was still wearing the clothes he'd been wearing earlier, and he looked so good, she had to take a deep breath to steady herself.

He came out to meet her and without a word, took her face in his hands and covered her lips with his, only releasing her when she was breathless and panting.

"I've been waiting to do that since I left your office," he said.

"Only that?" Hope teased.

He chuckled. "Why don't you come inside and find out?"

She took his outstretched hand, and as they walked toward the door, she noticed a brand-new

SUV among the other cars in the open garage. It was still covered with shipping foam and cellophane in some places.

"You had a new car delivered?" Hope said, mildly curious.

"Yeah, it's yours." He said offhandedly. "It arrived on Saturday. The keys are inside."

Hope stopped walking and raised her eyebrows. "You bought me a car?"

He shrugged.

"Were you going to tell me about it?"

"On Saturday? Of course? Right now, though...I confess it's not the uppermost thing in my mind. Getting you inside is."

"Too late!" Hope screamed, running to touch the car. She trailed her fingers over the glossy finish and ran back to Daniel, covering his face with kisses. "I love it! It's perfect."

"I know what you like," he said, watching her.

"Look at you being such a cool cat about buying a girl a brand new car," Hope teased. "You're not even raising your shoulder. You're just there like...I do this every day."

He laughed. "I don't...and it's only for you."

"I love you," she said, giving him another round of kisses. "Well, where are the keys? I'm taking it out for a spin."

Daniel groaned. "If you insist."

"Don't worry." She put her arms around him. "After the drive, you can still show me all the things you've been dying to show me since you left my office."

Much later, after she'd peeled off the foam and wrapping from the car and taken it on a drive around his neighbourhood, followed by dinner, and a few hours in his bed, they lay sated in each other arms.

"I don't know what I did to deserve you," Daniel told her. His arms tightened around her and he placed a kiss on her cheek.

"Are you for real?" Hope laughed. "I don't know what I did to deserve *you*."

"I can think of a couple of things," he teased, then buried his head in the crook of her neck and inhaled. "You smell incredible."

"You are incredible."

"I know," he gave her a lopsided grin, and she tossed a pillow at him. He swatted it aside, and she started to throw another one, but he covered her body with his, effectively restraining her. He grinned and kissed her nose. "I love you, Hope Alade."

She allowed herself to fall into his gentle gaze, his dark eyes. She'd never felt so loved as she did in that moment, so covered in strength, love, protectiveness and desire.

"I love you too." She kissed him. "I love everything you are."

He lay back on the bed. "What am I?"

"Strong, capable..." She sighed. In there was the boy who'd been abandoned by the woman who should have loved him more than anyone else in the world, but he'd moved past that and built a successful life for himself.

She put her hand on his arm. "Can I ask you something?"

He nodded.

"Did you ever see your mother, after she left?"

There was a long silence. "Not much to be honest. Her new husband worked internationally, and she was always abroad. So I never saw her, or my sister."

Hope squeezed his hand. "I'm sorry."

"It's okay." He shrugged. "You know...When I was twelve or so, she came to my school to visit. I was a boarder, and she knew the matron. They called me out of afternoon prep and she was waiting by her car." He chuckled sadly, remembering. "I'd told myself that I never wanted to see her again, that I didn't miss her. I'd stewed in my anger for so long, but the moment I saw her standing there by the car..." He shook his head. "It's still one of my happiest memories."

"It makes sense," Hope said. "You were a child, and she was still your mother."

"Oh well," He made a face. "We both cried. She got an exeat and took me out of school, bought me stuff, drove around, then she took me back. I asked if she was coming back home, she said no. I asked if I could come visit her, she said no. She dropped me at my hostel with enough provisions and gifts to last a year, and then she went away. I never saw her again. She died a year later in a car crash. Her husband was driving. He died too, along with their one-year-old son, a brother I didn't even know." He frowned. "His people didn't want Stephanie, so my dad brought her back home."

It was such an awful story. Hope put her arms around him. "I'm proud that you didn't let the pain keep you from being the wonderful person you are."

"I'm glad you think I'm a wonderful person."

Hope smiled. "I guess I'm biased. I love you, after all."

He laughed, then grabbed his watch from the nightstand and glanced at the time. "I should take you home."

"I can drive my new car?"

"I guess you can, but I'm coming with you."

"You're so protective." She paused. "I like it."

He kissed her again. "I'm glad."

"I wish I didn't have to leave...That's the thing about living with my parents."

He shrugged. "It's not like you'll be living at home for much longer."

"Hmm," Hope said absentmindedly. "I guess not."

Daniel gave her an enigmatic look but didn't say anything else on the subject. "You know it's really not that late. We don't have to go just yet."

Hope raised an eyebrow. "Really?"

He nodded. "Yes."

"So, what do you propose we do in the meantime?"

His grin was crooked. "I'll show you."

And he did.

EPILOGUE

It took a week to plan.

The idea had been brewing in Hope's mind since the day in the conference room, and after Daniel opened up more and more about his past, she felt more certain that it was the right thing to do.

She didn't doubt the intensity of Daniel's feelings for her, and her feelings for him were overwhelming, more than anything she'd ever experienced.

And even though she knew she didn't have to, she wanted to show him.

"Hey God!" Agnes exclaimed from beside her. "This is what they call risking it all. Are you sure we should go through with it?"

"We?" Hope asked, amused.

"I'm invested o." Agnes said. "Right now, I'm so tense. I feel as if I'm risking it all along with you."

"Don't worry, you're not." Hope smiled at her friend, though she was tense too, with excitement and many other emotions she couldn't quite name.

In a few moments, Daniel would emerge from the elevator. She'd told him to meet her in the lobby. As far as he knew, they were going out to dinner.

As far as he knew.

One elevator opened, and some people hurried out. No Daniel. Hope breathed.

"My heart..." Agnes said in a tense whisper.

Aside from the friends Hope had invited, there were a few other people in the lobby, closing from work, going home...if they wondered why Hope and Agnes were standing right in the middle of the marble space, they didn't say.

Another pair of elevator doors slid open and Daniel emerged.

He was such a god! Hope thought, her breath leaving her as she temporarily forgot why she was standing there. He was wearing one of his exquisitely tailored business suits, and he looked impeccable. It was hard to believe that he was all hers, but he was, every inch of him.

Her heart thudded. He looked up and saw her,

smiled, then started to saunter towards her. He took about four steps before the music started.

That was the first part. She'd arranged that with the building management and the security at the main reception.

Daniel stopped walking as Alicia Key's voice slid across the room like velvet.

His eyes met Hope's, a puzzled frown knitting his brow. She smiled at him and lifted the first card Agnes handed to her.

"I love you," it said.

She'd written all the cards earlier in the day, she lifted the next one.

You're perfect.

And the next, and the next.

You're strong, kind, and inspiring.

You're the man of my dreams.

You're smart.

You're sexy.

You make me happier than I've ever been before.

She was walking toward him, and Agnes, playing the loyal assistant, walked beside her, handing her the cards.

I want to grow old with you.

I want to share everything with you.

My joys. My pains. My life. My body.

My heart.

Forever.

That was the last card. Agnes handed Hope the last thing, a small box, then walked away to join the others. Hope's brother and sister, Daniel's friends, Uche, Dee, Ceecee, Temi, Briggs, his sister and brother. It had been a hassle to get them all here, and to keep it all a secret, but it was worth it. She needed to let him know, in front of the people that meant the most to them, how much he meant to her.

She was standing in front of him now, and he had a heartbreakingly tender expression on his face. She opened the box. The ring was a flat platinum band, with a filigree pattern chiselled in black along the surface. She met his gaze and grinned nervously.

"I love you," she whispered.

"I love you," he said.

She took a deep breath and pulled the ring out of its velvet bed, then she held his gaze and started to go down on one knee.

He caught her by the arms, "Don't—" he started, but they both lost their balance, and both ended up on their knees.

He was smiling, but Hope was too nervous to smile. "Daniel," she started.

"Yes," he said, and kissed her on her forehead, then on her lips.

"I haven't even asked," she said.

"Okay," he grinned. "Ask."

"Will you share the rest of your life with me?" she whispered.

"Absolutely," he replied softly. "Forever."

There was a buzz of conversation, clapping...but Hope couldn't hear a word. It was just her, and Daniel. He pulled her up with him as he rose. Then he kissed her again, this time it was long and lingering.

"I love you," he said when they stopped for air. His forehead was resting on hers. Then he took the ring and slid it onto his finger. He turned to their gathered friends and wiggled his fingers in the air.

There was an eruption of clapping and teasing. Daniel wrapped his arm around Hope's waist and pulled me to his side.

"Fiancée," he said.

She laughed. "I liked it, so I had to put a ring on it."

He looked around. "When did you arrange all this?"

"It wasn't easy," She admitted. "It took some planning. There's still the dinner at the restaurant later. Now that you've said yes, we're all going to stuff ourselves."

"Now that I've said yes," he laughed. "Was there any other possibility? You've made me a very happy man." He took her fingers in his. "Don't think this means I won't do something very elaborate and public when I put a ring on your finger."

"Really?" Hope teased. "A counter proposal?"

"I won't be outdone," he said, placing another kiss on her lips.

"Well, then." Hope returned the kiss. "I'm looking forward to it."

"THAT'S AN EXQUISITE RING."

Hope tore her gaze from her finger where the glittering cluster of sapphires and diamonds set on a pure platinum base winked and sparkled at her. She'd been hypnotised by the ring since the moment Daniel slipped it on her finger.

It hadn't been elaborate and public as he'd threatened. It had been romantic and beautiful, just the two of them in a beautiful city, in an apartment that was almost as high as the clouds. They'd been drinking wine and admiring the night sky when he'd quietly knelt and slipped the ring on her finger, with a silent question she'd answered with her eyes.

That was a few weeks ago, and after the engagement party, they were on holiday again, this time in the Bahamas.

"Thank you," Hope replied the woman with a polite smile.

"You look very happy," the woman continued, sipping from her drink in the poolside bar. "You must love him very much."

Hope chuckled. The words were much too tame to describe the depths of her feelings. "Yes," she said. "I love him very much."

At that moment, Daniel emerged from the pool. He was magnificent. With his tall athletic build and burnished skin, there was no ignoring him. Hope pulled in an anticipatory breath. It never got old, being with him. With every day that passed, her need for him intensified. He walked towards the bar, his eyes on her.

"Oh, that's him?" the woman beside Hope breathed. "Lucky you."

Yes, lucky me, Hope thought, abandoning her drink as she walked to meet Daniel.

He pulled her to him. "How's my wife?"

"We're not married yet," Hope reminded him.

He shrugged. "Soon enough. Just a few weeks and you'll be mine forever."

"I'm already yours." She ran her hands over the immense expanse of his chest. "It's kind of hot out here. I think we should go back to our bungalow."

He raised an eyebrow. "Why do I feel like it will get very hot in there?"

She walked past him, trailing her fingers down his arm, then turning back to give him a look under her lashes. "Because it is."

He held on to her hand, grinning.

"I love you Hope Alade-soon-to-be-Amadi. You're the only one for me."

Hope laughed. "Forever and Always."

He nodded in agreement. "Always."

The End.

FROM THE AUTHOR

Thank you for reading this book! I hope you enjoyed reading it as much as I enjoyed writing it. I have a thing for love and romance. I love it. I love stories about it, and I love creating those stories in my head.

When I was growing up, there weren't many love stories set in Nigeria, and, as a voracious reader, I read books set everywhere else, especially romances. It didn't feel right, because in Nigeria, we have stories, especially love stories.

Now, I write romance stories that could happen to people like me. The Only One is my third romance set in Nigeria, and there are many more to come, I promise.

If you've enjoyed this book, check out my other books at www.somiekhasomhi.com/books

Don't forget to leave a review.

ABOUT THE AUTHOR

Somi loves to read, and regularly dives into mythology, history, fantasy novels and old classics. She is a sucker for romance and can very often be found sighing over the exquisite love stories she consumes tirelessly.

In 2012, she started publishing the story that became Always Yours, as a blog serial at www.lagosromanceseries.com. It was later published as a novel. Her other books include Hidden Currents, the standalone sequel to Always Yours, as well as a short story, Jungle Justice.

She lives in Lagos, sometimes, and Houston at other times. When she's not writing or reading, she's either chasing her toddler around, mourning Daenerys Targaryen, or consoling herself with other TV shows and movies.

facebook.com/somiekhasomhi

twitter.com/somiekhasomhi

instagram.com/somivans

amazon.com/author/somiekhasomhi

goodreads.com/SomiEkhasomhi